# Raven

## *Reckoning MC Seer Book 3*

By BE Kelly

Raven (Reckoning MC Seer Book 3) Copyright © 2020 by BE Kelly.
Cover design: Lee Ching with Under Cover Designs
Imprint: Independently published

First Print Edition: March 2020
All rights reserved.

No part of this book may be reproduced, scanned, or distributed in any printed or electronic form without permission. Please do not participate in or encourage piracy of copyrighted materials in violation of the author's rights. Thank you for respecting the hard work of this author.

This is a work of fiction. Names, characters, places, and incidents either are the product of the author's imagination or are used fictitiously, and any resemblance to locales, events, business establishments, or actual persons—living or dead—is entirely coincidental.

## Table of Contents

| | |
|---|---|
| Remi | 1 |
| Jag | 9 |
| Texas | 13 |
| Remi | 18 |
| Jag | 27 |
| Texas | 41 |
| Remi | 51 |
| Jag | 64 |
| Texas | 72 |
| Remi | 81 |
| Texas | 93 |
| Remi | 101 |
| Jag | 115 |
| Texas | 127 |
| Remi | 137 |
| Jag | 148 |
| Remi | 160 |
| Texas | 185 |
| Jag | 193 |
| Remi | 205 |
| Texas | 218 |
| Remi | 230 |
| Oryana | 235 |
| Hawk | 239 |
| Ringer | 245 |
| Sophie | 250 |

# REMI

Remi walked into Reckoning and looked around the bar. She wasn't sure if she was crazy for going back there or just plain stupid, but she was pretty sure it was the latter. She had seen him again—Jag, and if she didn't get to him before midnight, she might be too late to save him. Remi looked around the crowded bar, hoping that she'd get lucky and spot either him or his friend, Texas.

"What are you doing here, Honey?" Tank asked. "You aren't supposed to be back in town for another couple weeks. Do Beth and Lyra know that you're home?" he asked. Remi had spent the last month in the desert, on a vision quest, as her grandmother liked to call them. It gave her an excuse to go home and visit with her aunt and grandmother for a few weeks and sort a few things out. When she got back from her visits home, she was usually refreshed and her mind was clear, but this time was different.

This time, while she was in the sweat lodge with her grandmother and aunt, she saw Jag and he was laying on the side of the road. Her Aunt Joanna had the same vision and even saw today's date. He had crashed his bike and from what Remi remembered seeing, he didn't make it. She couldn't let that happen. Not after he and Texas saved her life. She owed them both and if cutting her trip short to rush home and save Jag's ass was what she had to do, then so be it.

"No," she said. "I just got back into town and haven't had a chance to call either of them. I saw something and I think one of your guys needs help." She didn't miss the flash of concern on Tank's face.

"Who?" he asked. Having someone outright believe that she could see their future was kind of new to Remi. She usually had a whole lot of explaining to do to convince the person she was trying to help that she was on the up and up. Hell, the first time she met Lyra, she had to jump through hoops to get her to believe her and Lyra was a seer too.

"Jag," she almost whispered. Tank nodded to the corner of the bar where she spotted both Jag and Tex. They were playing darts and apparently not at a loss for female company. A pang of jealousy ran through her and honestly, she had no reason to feel that way. Jag and Texas made it very clear that they were both interested in her on her first visit to Reckoning. She was the one who turned them down, not sure that she was ready for what they were asking her to give them. Jag and Tex told her that they liked to share women and when they proposed that the three of them end up at Jag's place for the evening, she politely declined. They had asked a few other times, but each and every time, she found some lame excuse as to why she couldn't end up between the two of them. God, she wanted to agree to what they were asking her for but that would mean allowing herself some happiness in life and she couldn't let that happen.

Not since she lost her sweet Aria. She should have seen that drunk driver before even strapping her two-year-old daughter into the car and heading down the highway with her. She had seen countless other accidents and prevented them from happening, but she couldn't stop the unthinkable from happening to her own baby. No, she didn't deserve to have any happiness in her life—not anymore. For the most part, Remi was content with following her instincts and listening to her visions to help as many people as possible. It was her turn to pay back Jag's kindness and then she'd be on her way.

"Thanks, Tank," she muttered, stumbling around bikers and some barflies looking for a quick hook up, to make her way over to where Jag and Texas looked to be having a heated debate over who was closest to the bulls' eye. Remi picked up a dart and threw it at the board, hitting dead center.

"There you go, boys—settled it for you. I'm closest." Both guys turned around and the way they looked her over like they wanted her to be their next meal, made her rethink her trip into the bar. The blonde who had been hanging all over the two of them pouted at their lack of attention. She was at least bright enough to pick up the hint that she wasn't going to get what she wanted from either of them tonight and slunk back to the bar.

"Sorry about that, guys," Remi lied, nodding to where the pretty blonde started chatting up another biker. "She seemed like a sure thing."

"Why are you here, Remi?" Jag growled. She knew they hadn't parted on the best of terms. Remi was sure that turning them down so many times wore out her welcome, but she had no choice.

"I'm here to see you, Jag," she said.

"Well, fuck," Tex grumbled.

"It's not like that, Tex. I think you're in danger, Jag and I'd like to help," she said.

"In danger how? Stray dart or pretty blonde? Which one will be the end of me?" Remi knew he was being a smart ass but she had to admit, his remarks hurt her feelings. He had seen firsthand what she could do when she helped Lyra and Beth.

"Bike accident—off of highway twelve, tonight," she said.

"Damn," Texas said. "That's pretty specific, Honey."

"Well, I can only tell you what we saw and you can do with it what you'd like," she said.

"We?" Jag asked.

"Yeah, I went home and did a sweat lodge with my grandmother and aunt. My aunt saw today's date and I saw the accident and you lying on the side of the road."

"Fuck," Texas swore.

"You seem to be taking this better than your friend, Jag. Aren't you the least bit worried?" Remi asked. Jag shot Texas a look and they seemed to do the whole silent communication thing they were so good at.

"I'm not too worried about what you saw, Honey," Jag admitted. "I think you came here to help me change the outcome of your vision. Am I right?" he asked. Jag knew the score. He was the one who helped her and her sister, Nena find Lyra in that hospital room where the government guy was holding her. Jag was the one who found Remi some of Lyra's personal effects so she could get a read on her. Remi liked to hold something that belonged to the person when she was trying to see them. He had brought her one of Lyra's favorite pictures of her and her daughter, Delilah to hold onto. Seeing Lyra with her sweet little girl made her long for things that would never be for her and she wondered what Aria would look like as a six-year-old instead of being forever frozen in her mind as a precious toddler.

"I hope we can change the outcome of my vision, Jag. I think you are a nice guy and I'd hate to find you dead on the side of the road," she admitted. Jag's blue eyes looked at her as if he could see right through her. He shoved his overly long blond hair back from his face and smiled.

Jag laughed, "There ain't nothing nice about me, Honey. Hell, no one has ever accused me of being a nice guy in my life."

"Well, I see through your tough, biker routine, Jag. You and Tex both seem like stand-up guys and I'd like to help you." She knew she was laying it on a bit thick, but the idea of Jag getting on his bike and ending up as she saw him in her vision made her sick to her stomach.

"Thanks, Honey," Texas said, crowding up behind her. Jag flanked her front and Remi suddenly felt overheated and anxious to be on her way. They were both so different, not just in size but in demeanor. Jag was solid muscle but slimmer than Texas. His fair hair and blue eyes were her undoing and when he'd push up his sleeves to show off his tattoos, she wanted to drool. Tex was bigger than Jag and she knew he had to work out. He had fewer tats than Jag, but he still had a full sleeve up one arm. Tex's dark hair and eyes reminded her of the boys she used to date back home. He seemed familiar to her and she wondered if that was the reason why or if she had seen him in one of her visions and just didn't remember.

"I'm not too worried about your vision coming true, Honey," Jag admitted. He ran his hand down her arm, eliciting goosebumps every inch of the way.

"Wh—why's that?" she stuttered.

"Well," he teased, leaning into her body. "How about you repay your debt and save my life tonight?"

"That's what I'm trying to do," she said. "Save your life."

"Hmm, how far are you willing to go?" Texas whispered in her ear from behind.

"I don't understand," she said. "I traveled all the way back here from New Mexico if that's what you're asking."

Jag chuckled, "It's not, Honey. How about you come upstairs with Tex and I and let me thank you properly for your warning?" Tex crowded closer against her back and she was completely enveloped in warm, sexy men. The problem was Remi wasn't sure that she minded all that much.

"I already told you that I can't," she said.

"Alright," Jag barked. "Suit yourself. I'll just head on home then. Thanks for stopping by," he said, nodding to Texas and turning to leave.

"Did he mention he lives off of highway twelve?" Texas asked.

"Shit," Remi said. She watched as Jag said his goodbyes to some of the guys and Tank and she thought about letting the big jerk just walk out of the bar. She had done her duty and told him about her vision. Remi warned him and if he ended up dead on the side of the highway, that was on him—right? She sighed and followed him through the bar, knowing that no amount of internal reasoning with herself was going to work. She'd never win that argument. If she had to spend the night with two of the sexiest bikers she had ever met, to save one of their lives, then that was what she would do.

Jag was just about out the front door when she put her hand on his shoulder to stop him. "Jag, wait," she ordered. "I'll do it."

# JAG

"Do what, Remi?" he questioned, turning to face her; his sexy smirk in place.

"I'll go up to your room with you and Tex," she agreed. Texas was still behind her and Jag knew he had heard her.

"This has to be something you fully agree to," Jag said. "We won't force you to do anything."

"Except sleep with both of you to save your life," she grumbled. Texas chuckled from behind her and Jag shot him a look as if he wanted to tell him to shut the fuck up.

"She does have you there, man," Tex said. "But, he's right, Honey. If this is something you don't want, just say the word. I promise not to let Jag here go off and do something stupid to get himself killed—even if you tell us both no." Texas was right, but that didn't stop Jag from wanting to punch him for giving Remi an out.

The two of them had been working for weeks now to get her to agree to give them a chance. The first time he and Tex asked her if she'd be into the both of them taking her, she turned the cutest shade of red and politely declined. She was the most polished, polite woman he had ever met and God, she turned him completely inside out with her long, dark hair and brown eyes. Her Native American heritage intrigued him and her gift of being a seer, like Beth and Lyra, made him even more curious about the stranger who walked into Reckoning and changed all their lives.

Remi looked torn and Jag knew if he didn't act fast, she was going to take the easy way out of this and take Texas up on his offer to keep Jag from going off and getting himself killed. He was done waiting for her to make up her mind. They must have asked her a half dozen times to be theirs and she turned them down flat, each and every time. He could see the indecision in her dark eyes. Jag knew she was toying with the idea of agreeing to be theirs and now that she finally had, he wasn't going to let her change her mind. Not without a fight, at least.

"Don't change your mind, Honey," he begged. "I'll do whatever you tell me to do but don't renege on taking Tex and me up on our offer. Just give us one night—that's all. Then, you can be on your way and won't have to ever deal with us again." Remi looked between the two of them and damn if he didn't see a flash of disappointment in her eyes. It was giving him hope she'd say yes and one word from her now was all either of them would need to carry her up to the room, they rented from Tank, and make her theirs.

Jag could feel the excitement rolling off his friend's big body. He and Texas had known each other for years. When Jag got out of the military, Tex and he became fast friends. Women seemed to take notice of them both and when they'd go out to bars, Tex was his wingman. It took Jag longer to warm up to women and talking to them was more Tex's thing than his. Women seemed to really like his friend and when Tex came up with the idea to share them, Jag thought he was crazy. The first time they shared a woman seemed to work for them and the two of them had been doing it ever since. Tex was the smooth talker that women seemed to like and he was the alpha, barking orders and making sure everyone had what they needed from their night together.

It worked for them and when Remi strolled into Reckoning, Texas got that same look in his eyes—the one that told Jag that he wanted her and usually that was all it took. But, Remi gave poor Tex a run for his money and seeing his friend, standing behind her, suffering in silence was almost comical.

"Come on, Remi," Jag begged. "If not for me, then do it for poor Tex," he said. "I mean, just look at the guy. He's wanted you for months now." Remi looked over her shoulder to Texas and smiled and then turned back to face Jag. She was so close; he could feel her warm breath on his cheek.

"How about you, Jag?" she questioned. "Do you want me?"

"I do," he breathed. "More than I want my next breath." Admitting that to her was easy because it was true.

"If I agree to this," she said. "It will only be for one night and I'm only doing it to save your life and stop my vision from happening." Remi looked between them and Jag smiled over her shoulder to Texas.

"What do you say, brother?" he asked.

"I say fuck yeah," Texas said, making them both laugh.

"Can I at least get a drink before we head up to your room?" Remi asked. Jag wanted to be a complete ass and deny her request but he nodded.

"Shots," he agreed. "They work faster and we can get you upstairs. Times wasting, Remi," he said. She giggled as if he was joking but he wasn't. If she was only giving him and Texas one night, he didn't want to waste a second of it. They had both waited too long for the dark-haired raven who mysteriously changed their lives and in his case—saved him.

# TEXAS

Texas watched as Remi drank her shot in one swallow, her long neck thrown back as she downed the liquid courage. He knew she was nervous about spending the night with them and he had to admit, he was too. Tex hadn't wanted a woman, really wanted one, for so long, but when Remi walked into Reckoning, a few months back, he nearly swallowed his damn tongue.

She was his walking wet dream but there was more to it than that. He felt oddly drawn to Remi and if he wasn't mistaken, Jag felt the same way about her. Texas wasn't blind; he noticed the way his best friend watched the raven-haired beauty. His eyes never left her every time they were in the same room together and tonight was no exception. If she followed through with her promise to spend the night with them, there would be no way that either of them would let her walk away again. They already made that mistake once—the night that they went in to rescue her and her twin sister, Oryana.

Remi had been looking for Nena for weeks and when she finally caught up to her, it was almost too late for both of them. Remi had walked right into a trap and if Lyra hadn't called to tell them about her dream, of seeing Nena and Remi locked away in that warehouse, he and Jag might have lost her.

Texas knew the score—women liked him because he was a sweet talker and they liked that. When it came to looks, he'd never be able to compete with Jag. He was usually fine with that but seeing the way Remi looked at Jag made him feel things he'd never had to deal with before. The worst being jealousy; which was crazy since Jag was his best friend in the whole world. Tex met Jag just after he got out of the military. His friend was broken and needed a wingman and he was happy to be that for him. Things eventually turned into more than him just talking up his best friend. Women were agreeing to be with them both and Jag seemed to like the idea. Texas was always up for some fun and sharing women with Jag just felt right. Remi was no exception, but Tex was going to have to work harder to tamp down his green-eyed monster before things got too out of hand. The last thing he wanted to do was take his jealousy out on either of them. That wasn't what this was about. Remi had finally agreed to give them a chance and he needed to concentrate on that fact and leave the rest of his baggage at the door.

She followed them up to the room that he and Jag rented from Tank. It was easier to take women there instead of introducing them to where they really lived. It was also a whole lot less messy when they'd try to track down him or Jag, wanting another turn with the two of them. That wasn't the way they liked to play things. Remi smirked up at him and shook her head. "How many women do you two bring up here?" she questioned, as if able to read his thoughts.

"What exactly are your abilities, Honey?" Texas asked. If she could read minds, he was pretty sure that he and Jag both were fucked. Hell, if she could read minds, this might all have gone a lot smoother than it had between the three of them.

"No," Remi giggled. "I can't read minds, Tex. But, it's not hard to decipher what the two of you are thinking."

"How's that?" Jag questioned.

"Well, you two tell it like it is. You've been completely open about what you want from me and I'm betting I'm not the first woman you've asked to do this—you know sharing thing, with." Remi looked between the two of them as if expecting them to give her an answer to the question she really never asked.

"If you're asking if we've shared women before, then the answer is yes," Texas said. "We don't hide the fact that we like to share women. If you're not up to this, just say so, and this all ends here and now." Texas felt like he was holding his damn breath, waiting for her to make up her mind again. It was like watching a ping pong match, trying to keep up with her. His fingers flexed on the doorknob where they rested, waiting to hear her final verdict.

"I'm here, Texas and I agreed to this. I'm not going to renege now," she mumbled. Tex worried that they were pushing Remi into something she might regret and he hated that. She was an honorable woman, trying to help people with her abilities and now, Jag was on the receiving end of her kindness. Texas would do just about anything to keep his friend from ending up the way he had in Remi's vision. What he wouldn't do was force her to be between the two of them.

Texas nodded and turned the doorknob, letting the door swing open. A single king-sized bed sat in the middle of the room and he watched Remi as she took in the sparse furnishings. Remi smiled and looked up at him again.

"You guys travel light," she teased. "Honestly, all you need is a neon sign flashing the words, 'bachelor pad' and this place will be the complete package." Jag choked back his laugh and crossed the room to close the blinds.

"Well, the secrets out," he said. "Tex and I are two single men who like to share women. She's found us out," he teased. Remi giggled again and it was so nice to hear her finally happy. Texas wasn't sure if they would ever see that side of her. Between warning Lyra about Dave and tracking down her sister, Texas was sure she didn't have much to laugh about in life. There was more though. Every time he looked at her, he could feel her sadness and Texas knew it had more to do with anything that was going on around them. Remi had been through something —something awful and he wondered if she'd ever let him in and share that part of herself with either of them.

"Ready," Remi defiantly asked, raising her chin as if daring either of them to turn her away now. It wouldn't happen, not now or ever, but Texas wasn't about to tell her that. He planned on taking whatever Remi was willing to give them and, in the process, slowly chip away at the giant wall she had built around herself. Sooner or later, she'd let him in—she'd let them both through her barrier.

## REMI

She felt like a rebellious child, staring down Jag and Texas as if challenging either of them to change their minds. Remi was awkward and completely out of her element. She tried to act cool, resting her hands on her hips, as if channeling her inner angry librarian, but that didn't seem to fly with the guys. Maybe they didn't spend much time in libraries or maybe they just didn't find her as threatening as the town's residents. As far as librarians went, she hardly fit the mold but not fitting into the roles people generally tried to place her in, was kind of her thing. There really weren't many Native American librarians in her town and that was just fine with her. Remi liked being different and besides her twin sister, Oryana, not many people got her.

Remi made a show of checking her watch as if letting Jag and Texas know she wasn't going to wait all night. "We going to do this guys?" she asked. "I have to be at work in ten hours and will need to run home to shower, change and feed my cats."

"Cats," Jag asked. "As in more than one?"

"Yep," she proudly said. "Five, actually."

"You have five cats?" Texas questioned.

"Yep," Remi said. Texas and Jag shared a look and then actually had the nerve to laugh. "Um, what's so funny?" she asked.

"Just that, with that many cats, you could be considered an old, crazy cat lady," Jag teased.

"Yeah, but she definitely doesn't fit the old and frumpy part of it," Texas said, correcting Jag's assessment of her. "How about the crazy part, Honey? You fit that part of the description?" Texas asked.

"Well, that depends on the situation. Like, right now, dealing with you two—I'm feeling a little crazy," Remi teased. "Maybe this was a bad idea." Remi picked up her bag and headed for the door.

"Don't," Jag ordered. "You promised that you won't back out of our deal, Remi," he said. He sounded more desperate than angry and Remi knew exactly how he felt. Every time she turned the guys down, she felt a pang of desperation that would have her running all the way back to her grandmother's house in New Mexico. Her Anali, as Remi called her in her native Navajo language, could always tell when she was running from something rather than just making a trip home for a visit.

Remi turned back to face Jag, noting the panic she saw in his eyes. "Alright," she whispered. She crossed the small room and wrapped her arms around Jag's neck. "I'll stick around, but you need to figure out what you're going to do with me. You do have just one night," she reminded him.

"So you said," Jag teased. He looked around her body to where Texas stood in the corner of the room. "What should we do with her, Tex?" Jag asked.

Texas closed the distance between them and wrapped his arms around Remi, her back to his front. She could feel his erection pressing into her back, letting her know that she wasn't the only one affected by what seemed to be playing out between the three of them. "I'm pretty sure we can figure out a few things," Texas drawled.

Jag kissed his way up her neck and when he got to her lips, he stopped to watch her, as if silently asking her permission. Texas tugged her long, dark hair to one side and kissed her neck, gently nibbling her shoulder. They were good at working together to distract her, but Remi was guessing they had a good deal of practice with sharing a woman.

"What are you waiting for, man?" Texas asked.

Jag smiled at her and nearly took her breath away. "I'm waiting for our Raven to give me the go-ahead," Jag said. "Tell me I can kiss you, Remi."

Remi wasn't sure if she liked that he called her his Raven. Honestly, the name hit a little too close to home. Her Anali had always called her the all-seeing Raven and Remi wondered how Jag had picked up on that.

"How do you know my nickname?" she stuttered.

"What?" he whispered. His lips were so close to hers; she could practically feel them brush against her own. She wanted him to kiss her. Hell, she wanted them both to make her theirs, but first, she needed some answers. Remi never took signs and little coincidences lightly. They were too important and to people like her—women who could see things, both past, and future, they could mean the difference between life and death.

"You called me Raven," she said, leaning into Jag's big body. She couldn't help herself, letting her fingers trace his tattoos and lean muscles up his forearms. "That's my nickname."

"Really?" he asked. Jag seemed surprised and Remi took a step back from him, pressing tighter against Texas' body. She reached for the hem of her t-shirt and tugged it over her head, leaving her standing between the two of them in just her bra and jeans. She liked the way Texas let his hands freely roam her body. He wouldn't be asking her for her verbal consent at every turn of their night together. She had already given him the green light by agreeing to go to their room with them and that seemed to be enough for Texas. Jag, on the other hand, needed more reassurances that she was a willing participant in tonight's debaucheries. Jag looked her torso over, letting his eyes rest on what she wanted him to see—her tattoo of a raven on her upper shoulder. The bird looked almost as if it was flying through her body and Texas let his fingers trace the part of the tat that ran along her back shoulder blade.

"A raven," he whispered.

"How did you know?" she asked Jag again.

He shrugged and gave her his easy smile. "We didn't," he admitted. "Texas and I just got to talking about you one night and well, we both agreed that nickname fit you. Hell, I can't really explain it."

"I can," she said. "We have a connection, the three of us," she admitted. It was something she always looked for in other people. Usually, when she found a strong connection with others, especially men, she ran the opposite way. Remi didn't have time for messy relationships that she knew from experience would only lead to heartache.

"I don't know about that," Jag countered. "I mean—it could just be that we are good guessers and hell, maybe it's just a coincidence."

"No such thing," she challenged.

"As a coincidence?" Jag asked.

"Nope," she said. "I don't believe in them or in fate," she said. "I've learned that people's paths are usually changed by the choices they make. For example, when I showed up here tonight, to save your life," she paused and smiled up at him as if reminding Jag that she had a purpose for just showing up at Reckoning. "I changed your fate by agreeing to spend the night with the two of you."

"Okay," Texas said. "We get the whole change the outcome thing. When you helped us to save Lyra, it changed what she saw. You can't honestly believe that coincidences don't exist. How do you explain chance meetings or bumping into someone you were just thinking about a few days before?"

"I see those as the universes way of putting us in the right place at the right time. Maybe you weren't supposed to go to the grocery store, but you realized the milk in your refrigerator was spoiled, leaving you no choice. While you're there, you run into an old high school friend who had been having a hard time with life. You ask your old friend to dinner and she accepts and while you're at dinner, she tells you that she was planning on going home tonight and was going to kill herself because she felt so completely alone. Her chance meeting at the grocery store reminded her that someone in the world cares and she changed her mind. Instead of ending her life, she decides to go to see a therapist to get help for her depression," Remi paused and smiled at Jag. "After two years of therapy, you see her again at the same supermarket. This time, she's happy. She tells you that she's married to her former therapist and they are expecting their first child together. How can that be just a coincidence or something that happened by chance?"

"Wow," Jag breathed.

"Yeah, wow," she agreed. "It's a true story. The universe put me in her path, not coincidence." Jag held up his hands as if in defeat. "Okay, Honey. I get it—no such thing as fate or coincidence. But how would I know about your tattoo or nickname?"

That was something Remi couldn't explain. She knew that she was connected to them both, in some way. It's why she felt as if she knew Texas and why she was seeing Jag's path. Remi usually had a connection to the people she saw in her premonitions and the bond that seemed to exist between the three of them scared her—though she wasn't about to tell them that.

Remi shrugged and smiled. "No clue," she admitted. Texas wrapped his arms around her almost naked body, reminding her that she was standing in front of them wearing only her bra and jeans.

"I like the idea of the three of us being connected," he admitted. Remi wrapped her arms over his, hugging him close.

"Me too, Tex." Remi looked at Jag and nodded. "You can kiss me, Jag," she whispered. For just a split second, Jag looked confused. She could tell the exact moment he seemed to catch up, taking a step towards her, invading her personal space. Jag leaned into her body and gently brushed his lips over hers. He was so gentle with her, compared to Texas. He seemed almost shy when it came to taking what he wanted from her and when he touched her, it felt like he was making her promises. But, that was crazy. He wasn't promising her anything except a night together and that was all she was capable of giving either of them in return.

"My turn," Texas growled, turning her in his arms. Remi ran her hands up over his shoulders, hooking her hands behind his neck. She was tall but next to Texas and Jag, she almost felt petite.

"Yes," she agreed. "Your turn, Tex." He smiled a wolfish grin at her, making her giggle. He pulled her tighter against his body and didn't hesitate. Texas kissed her like he was a starving man, licking and nipping his way into her mouth. Remi moaned and he took that as his cue to deepen their kiss. Jag pressed up against her back and she had never felt so safe, surrounded by their big bodies. But it was more than just having them close. Remi could feel that they had been waiting for her, wanting her for so long and now that she was agreeing to let them take what they wanted from her, she felt like the universe might be trying to tell her something. What that might be, she had no idea. Sometimes, the clues were so loud she instantly knew what she was meant to do. With Texas and Jag, it felt like the universe was screaming at her in a language she couldn't understand and that scared the shit out of her. For the first time in a damn long time, Remi was flying blind and finally taking what she wanted. What could possibly go wrong?

# JAG

Jag wasn't sure how much more teasing he could take. Remi was driving him to the brink of insanity and watching her with Texas was making him feel things he hadn't usually experienced—namely jealousy. That emotion was a new one for him when it came to him and Texas sharing women. Then again, he had never wanted a woman as badly as he did Remi.

Jag was ex-military and that afforded him the type of lifestyle he always dreamed of having. He joined the Air force to become a pilot and see the world, just like the stupid brochures promised. He just never imagined he'd enlist and be sent into a warzone that was a hotbed for shooting down American fighter jets. He was one of the lucky ones—he got out. Some of his buddies weren't so lucky and once his time was up, he refused to re-up no matter how much the military offered him, trying to make it worth his while. He was thirty-four years old and had too much life to live to fight someone else's war.

Once he got back home, he realized he had nothing waiting for him. No woman was sitting back in the states, hoping he'd make it back to her safely. Jag moved down to New Orleans from his hometown of Michigan. It wasn't just a temperature change, but a culture shock for him. He had one friend in the world he knew he could reach out to and that was Tank. He and Tank had known each other in the service and when he decided to take the leap and move to NOLA, he called his buddy. He helped Jag get settled and when he wanted to prospect for Reckoning, Tank found him a sponsor—Reaper. They were his family now—his brothers and he was damn lucky to have each of them in his life.

He loved his life in NOLA. Jag had enough money saved up to buy an eighteen passenger plane and he started up his own venture of running local businessmen from state to state. They liked the anonymity he afforded them and the fact that they could basically fly private without the cost of owning their own jet. He made a damn good living catering to the rich and sometimes even famous clientele who called NOLA home.

When he met Texas, he almost wrote the guy off. Tex was a kid from the wrong side of the tracks and Jag didn't want to get mixed up with him. He had done time for stealing a car when he was just nineteen. Texas started coming around Reckoning when he got out of prison and Jag tried to tell the guy to get lost, but Tex never took his not so subtle hints. Texas was as decent as they came. He spent five long years in prison, making up for one stupid mistake and he deserved a chance. They were the same age and Jag could see a lot of himself in the guy. Texas grew on him over time and when he asked Jag to be his sponsor, to prospect into Reckoning, he agreed. The two had been inseparable over the past five years and Jag never felt anything but respect and admiration for his friend. Seeing Texas with Remi tonight evoked all new feelings though and Jag wondered if it was all worth it—if she was worth it.

"You good man," Texas questioned as if he could pick up on Jag's feelings of unease.

"Yeah," he lied.

Remi smiled up at him and shook her head, making a tsking noise. "You aren't a very good liar," she accused.

"What makes you think I'm lying, Honey?" Jag countered. He and Remi didn't really know each other. She had been to Reckoning a handful of times when she was trying to save Tank's woman, Lyra. He had to admit, he and Texas had more than one conversation about the sexy dark haired raven who walked into Reckoning and turned the both of them inside out with lust. But, she was determined to give them hell, turning them down every chance she got. Jag didn't believe they'd ever get their shot with her and there was no way in hell he'd fuck this all up now.

Remi shrugged, "I feel it," she said. He knew she had the same special powers that Lyra and her sister Beth had. Remi and her twin sister, Oryana seemed to have different skill sets than Lyra and Beth. Jag knew enough to know that if Remi said she could sense something; he should believe her.

Remi placed her palms flat against his chest as if she was trying to feel his heart beating through his shirt. Hell, she could probably feel it racing since he felt like it was going to beat out of his damn chest. And, when she looked at him, it was as if Remi could see straight through him—right into his soul. She closed her eyes and smiled.

"You don't want to share me with Texas," she said.

"What the fuck," Texas growled. Remi turned and put one palm flat against Texas' chest and giggled.

"You feel the same way," she said. "You can't tell me that jealousy hasn't played into your feelings before. You share women, so you must have gotten jealous, watching each other before."

"No," Jag breathed. "Never."

"Me either," Texas admitted. "Why now, Jag?" he asked. That was the million-dollar question here. Why was he suddenly getting all worked up about having to share a woman with his best friend? Tex was his wingman, the one person he could turn to for anything and he knew Texas would be there for him, no matter what it cost him personally. Jag knew that Texas had given up things he wanted in his own life, to stay in New Orleans to be a part of Jag's life and their club, Reckoning. He had overheard his friend's conversations with his foster parents, back home in Arizona, begging him to just come home. Tex always came up with some excuse as to why he couldn't make the trip home but Jag wondered if it wasn't because of him. Tex could move back to Arizona and make a fresh start but he chose to stay with Jag. Texas stuck around and Jag often worried that he was holding his friend back by not insisting that he move back home.

Jag even thought of letting the guy off the hook and moving back to Michigan. He knew he'd have the love and support of his parents and his three older brothers. Jag sometimes envied Tex not having such a big family. Sure, he'd give his life for them but they stuck their noses in his business and Jag hated that. It was one of the reasons he hadn't been home in a few years and why he only called his parents on holidays. He hoped that the distance would make them back off some, but he was wrong. It only made his parents more interested in what he had going on. How was he supposed to explain the fact that he and Tex shared women? His family would never understand and staying away was his best option.

"I don't know," Jag admitted. "But, I think it's something I can work through." He wasn't sure if that was the truth or a lie, at this point. He wanted to at least try because they might not get another chance at having Remi between them again.

"Me too," Texas admitted. "I've been feeling this way all night and I was beginning to worry that something was wrong with me. I'd like to try too," Tex said.

"You two have more drama than most women I know," Remi teased. She was still standing between the two of them, her arms outstretched and her palms flat against each of their chests. Jag liked the way her fingers flexed in his shirt as if Remi was telling him that she needed more. Jag took that as his cue to give her what she seemed to need; show her what she'd be working with. He yanked his black t-shirt up over his head, leaving his chest bare and Texas did the same. Remi let her hands freely roam both of their bodies and he had to admit, it felt damn good having her touch him. Jag moaned and leaned into Remi's soft touch.

"That feels so good, Baby," Jag praised.

"He's right," Texas agreed. "You touching me feels like Heaven." Jag watched as Texas pulled Remi into his arms and he couldn't help himself, he stood behind her, framing her body with both of theirs. He wanted to mark her, make her his, but most of all, he wanted to possess Remi.

Jag stood and watched as Tex kissed Remi and he felt a searing fire rip through his sole. He'd never felt so possessive or protective of a person as he did Remi. He needed to get his fucking head on straight if this was going to work between the three of them and right now, he wanted nothing more.

Texas shot him a smug smile over Remi's shoulder and Jag wanted to punch it off his fucking face. "She tastes so good," he taunted. Jag growled and spun Remi around to face him, causing Texas to laugh.

"My fucking turn," Jag growled. He kissed his way into her mouth and damn if Tex wasn't right. Remi did taste damn good and Jag wasn't sure he'd ever get enough of her. One night wasn't going to be enough for him and he was pretty fucking certain that it wouldn't be enough for Texas, judging from the way he was watching Jag kiss Remi.

He broke their kiss, leaving Remi panting for air. "Why do I get the feeling that you two are going to tear me apart before this is all over? You boys think you can behave or should we quit before we even get started?" She smiled up at him, but Jag could see the fear behind her teasing. Remi was afraid of something and Jag worried that it might involve the way the two of them were pawing at her, fighting over who was going to take her first.

"Sorry, Honey," he said. "How about if we promise to check our jealousy and you let us show you just how well we don't behave?" He felt like he was holding his fucking breath, waiting for her to give him an answer. There was no way that he wanted her to call this thing quits. Jag wanted his chance with Remi and if he had to man up and push his jealousy down, he'd do just that.

"I'm not sure this is a good idea," Remi whispered. "But, I honestly don't care. I've wanted you two for so long now, I think walking away would be a mistake. Besides, it's not yet midnight and if you leave now, my vision might become a reality. I can't let that happen, Jag," she murmured. He nodded, but a part of him wanted answers. Namely, if she was just agreeing to their night together to save his life or if she honestly wanted them, like she just admitted.

"Who's taking lead?" Texas asked. When the two of them shared women, they would usually decide beforehand who was going to play alpha. Usually, that was Jag's part but tonight was different. Their dark-haired raven had surprised them, walking into Reckoning from out of the blue and they hadn't had the time to discuss their plan of action. Having one of them take lead helped with confusion and it usually led to them, and the woman they brought up to their room, having one hell of a good time together.

Remi giggled, crossing the small room to sit down on the bed. She was still wearing only her bra and jeans and watching her walk around that way made Jag nearly want to swallow his damn tongue.

"What's so funny, Baby?" Texas drawled.

Remi pointed to the pair of them, "You two," she admitted. "Do you always plan who's going to be in charge when it comes to sex?" She threw herself back onto the bed, letting her fits of giggles rack her body.

"Fucking great," Jag complained. "We finally get the woman we've been literally dreaming about, to agree to come up to our fucking room, and she's laying on our bed laughing at us. This really isn't how we planned it," he grumbled. It wasn't either. For months now, he had been dreaming of Remi giving them a night —just one night—to prove that the three of them could work and here he was fucking everything up. In his nightly fantasies, she would agree to everything they demanded of her, gifting them both with her complete submission. But, the woman who was currently rolling around on their bed showed no signs of being submissive. In fact, he was sure that Remi didn't have a submissive bone in her sexy body.

"Shit," Texas swore. Remi sat up and tried, really tried, to sober. "He's right," Texas said. "We've both wanted this for so long and now, we're fucking it all up." Texas crossed the room and stood over Remi's body. "You good with obeying both of us?" Texas questioned.

Jag groaned and Remi looked about ready to bust out into fits of laughter again. "Obey?" she squeaked.

"Yeah," Tex barked as if he didn't understand her questioning him. "Obey—as in taking orders. Which one of us do you want to give the orders, Honey?" Remi smiled up at him, biting back her giggle.

"Um, I'm really not the kind of girl to take orders from anyone, Texas," she sassed, resting her hands on her slender hips.

"She's not submissive," Jag said. "Look at her man, Remi doesn't take orders, she fucking gives them." Texas looked her up and down and Jag felt about ready to join Remi and fall onto the bed laughing at his friend's expression.

"You're not submissive?" Texas asked. Remi shook her head, not taking her eyes off the big guy, as if challenging him to give her any argument.

"Nope," she breathed. "I didn't know that was a prerequisite for following you guys up here. Listen, if this is a deal-breaker for you, Texas—" Remi found her shirt on the floor and picked it up to slip over her head.

"No," they both said in unison. He could hear Texas' panic. It was the same that he felt—a gnawing, savage feeling to take Remi. They wouldn't let her just walk out of that room. Yeah, they were both animals when it came to it and Jag's desires for Remi were downright primal.

"We can make this work," Jag offered. Remi dropped her shirt back to the floor and sauntered across the room to where he stood. He couldn't seem to take his eyes off the way she playfully swayed her hips. Yeah, she knew exactly what she was doing and how to play the game.

"Down on your knees," she ordered. Jag looked across the room to Texas and he wasn't sure what his next move should be. The defiant smirk on his friend's face told him that Tex wouldn't so easily bend to Remi's demands. Jag, on the other hand, was willing to do some fucking bending if that would end with her screaming out his damn name. Jag sunk to his knees and Remi gifted him with her sly smile. Remi thrust her hips in his direction and his dick twitched at what she was offering him. Jag leaned in to inhale her scent and even through her jeans, he could tell that she was completely turned on by the whole scene.

"Fuck, Baby," Jag swore. He looked past Remi to the corner of the room to find Tex still watching them. He wanted to tell his friend to get his head out of his ass and give her what she wanted from them but Texas didn't look like he was willing to give an inch on the matter. His friend craved dominance and letting Remi take that from him might be too much for poor Texas.

"She smells so good, Texas," he whispered, wrapping his big hands around her slender hips to pull her against his face. He wanted to do more than just smell her. God, he wanted to touch her and the thought of tasting her made his mouth water.

"This isn't us," Texas drawled. "We don't get on our fucking knees, she does."

Jag sighed and nodded. "I'm sorry, Remi," he said. "You're going to have to give Texas a minute to catch up with the current century. His inner caveman is butt hurt that you won't play by his rules." Remi giggled and Tex made a scoffing noise from the corner of the room. He slunk down into the room's only chair and crossed his ankle over his knee. Jag knew his friend well. He knew that Tex was trying for laid back and easy-going, but the erection he was sporting told a different story.

Remi looked back over her left shoulder and smiled. "Suit yourself, Tex," she offered. She turned back to face Jag and flashed her wicked grin. "Get me naked and eat my pussy," she ordered. Jag didn't even hesitate this time. Hearing her ask for —no, demand—what she wanted was so fucking hot. Jag unzipped her skin-tight jeans and worked them down her body, pulling her lacy panties down with them. After he helped her to step clear of her jeans, he kissed his way up her body, practically shoving his nose into her already drenched pussy. Jag made a humming noise in the back of his throat and he almost felt bad for Tex when he heard his soft curses coming from the corner of the room. He could hear Texas shifting in the chair behind Remi and if Jag wasn't mistaken, he heard him unzip his jeans.

"Poor Texas," Remi said, pouting out her bottom lip. "You want to play so badly, but you don't know how to ask nicely. Ask me, Tex. Ask me to play with us," she ordered. Jag kissed his way up Remi's body, almost demanding her attention back on him. He stood in front of her and unhooked her bra, letting her ample breasts fill his hands. Remi moaned and thrust them against his palms.

"Yes," she hissed. "More, Jag," Remi insisted. "I need more." Jag walked her back to the bed, pushing her down as soon as the back of her knees hit the mattress. She willingly fell onto the bed and spread her legs, as in invitation.

She didn't have to tell him what she wanted him to do next. Jag settled between her legs and licked her wet folds, sucking her sensitive clit into his mouth. She practically screamed out his name, running her hands through his hair, tugging on the ends. Remi was aggressive and bossy; everything he thought he'd never want in a woman. Now, with her in his bed, letting him eat her pussy, shouting out his fucking name—he'd never want anything or anyone else.

## TEXAS

Tex stroked his heavy shaft in his own damn hands, wishing it was Remi's touch he was feeling. Earlier, when she so freely touched his body, it felt like he was coming home. How could he have missed the signs that she wasn't submissive? It really wasn't a deal-breaker for him, but letting a woman take control wasn't something he usually let happen. The question was would he be able to walk away from Remi now? He wanted her —God, he fucking wanted her and watching Jag eat her out was just about driving him out of his damn mind.

Hearing Remi scream out Jag's name as she came on his mouth made him want to give up his stubborn pride and give her exactly what she wanted. Tex just wanted her to meet him half-way, a little give and take, but that wasn't something Remi seemed interested in. Hell, maybe this was Remi's plan all along. Sometimes, when it was just the three of them hanging out, Texas got the feeling that Remi was more into Jag than she was him. Maybe she wanted Jag to be the one joining her in bed and this was just her way to make sure that happened. She had to know that Texas wasn't going to give up his dominance so easily. It wasn't how things were done in his world. Remi had been around their MC world enough to know that bikers weren't the type to drop to their fucking knees just because a sexy as shit woman demanded it. Well, that's what he thought until Jag sunk to his knees as soon as the seer demanded it. It was as if his friend was under Remi's spell and honestly, he felt the same damn way.

"Texas," Remi begged. "Please." She reached across the bed towards him and he had to look away from the two of them. It was too much and if he gave in now, he'd be giving up everything. Texas was worried that not giving in would have the same ending—him losing everything and walking out of the damn room without having the woman who haunted his dreams for months now. He wanted her too much to do that. He needed to taste her, mark her and make her his or he might regret sitting this one out for a damn long time.

"Don't be like this, man," Jag warned. "You know you want her. Remi isn't asking for anything you're not willing to give. Come taste her," Jag begged. "Make her ours with me."

"Fuck," Texas swore. Jag was right, but that shouldn't really surprise him. Jag was always fucking right.

"I want you, Texas," Remi begged.

"But, not enough to let me be in charge," Texas said. He sounded like a complete ass, but he couldn't help it. It was who he was.

"How about a compromise?" Remi offered. "You come over here, tell me what you want and I'll do my best to give that to you." Remi looked so hopeful, he almost wanted to laugh. Jag stripped and was standing over her body, sending him pleading looks. Texas sighed and stood, shucking out of his jeans.

"Fine," he growled.

Remi's giggle filled the room. "Gee Tex, don't seem so happy about fucking me," she teased.

"I'm sure he's just sexually frustrated, Baby. Maybe you can help him out?" Jag asked. Texas didn't need his friend to fucking beg Remi to give him anything. He could ask for what he wanted and if she was willing to give it, fine. Otherwise, he'd finish jerking himself off and Jag and Remi could figure things out without him.

"Don't do me any favors," Texas grouched.

Remi laughed again and he stroked his own cock, loving the way her eyes followed his movement. "How much are you willing to compromise, Honey?" Texas asked.

"Wh—why are you asking me that?" Remi asked, eyeing him suspiciously.

"Are you willing to get down on those pretty knees for me?" he almost whispered. Remi smiled up at him and it felt like the whole damn room lit up.

"Yes," she said, enthusiastically nodding her agreement.

"Alright," Texas said. "How about we put that bossy mouth of yours to work then, Honey," he taunted. Remi slid off the bed and down to the floor, kneeling in front of him and he didn't hide his appreciation.

"Thank you for this, Honey. You are so fucking beautiful." Remi smiled up at him and opened her mouth as if offering everything he was asking her for. Texas stroked his big hand down her beautiful cheek, cupping her jaw. Remi wrapped her hands around his cock and let her tongue playfully dart out to lick the tip of his dick. Texas hissed out his breath and she sucked his cock into her hot mouth, moaning out her pleasure. She was a vixen, his siren, the person he had been chasing for months and he'd finally caught her. A part of Tex wondered if he would ever truly catch her. He had a feeling that would depend on when or even if Remi Nez wanted to be caught. He wanted to believe he was taking control of the situation, but that couldn't be further from the truth. He was the exact opposite of in control, but he wasn't ready to tell Remi that. Admitting that he was completely out of control wasn't something he wanted to admit to either person standing in front of him. Remi let his cock pop free from her lips and Tex instantly missed her warm mouth around his dick.

Jag sat down on the edge of the bed as if needing a front-row seat to watch the two of them. Remi turned back to Jag to run her hand over his erection. His friend moaned and thrust into her hands, taking the pleasure she was offering him.

"Please, don't stop," Jag begged Remi. She stood and wrapped her arms around Jag's shoulders. "I won't," Remi promised. "I need you," she admitted. Remi turned to Texas to take his hand into hers. "Both of you." Hearing Remi say that she wanted them both did crazy things to his heart. It was what Texas had been waiting for, even if he didn't know it. He wanted her to give him the words and now that she had, Tex wanted nothing more than to make Remi his.

He and Jag surrounded her, touching and kissing her. They were a mesh of hands, lips, and tongues and all Texas could think about was sinking into her willing body to hear Remi whisper his name on her lips.

Texas walked her back to the bed and nudged her back down onto the mattress. He wanted to make her pretty promises, but that wasn't what tonight was about. Tonight was three people finally getting what they needed from each other. It was about taking the pleasure Remi was willing to give to them both. That's just what Texas was going to give her too. He didn't give Remi any warning, just sank into her body, balls deep, loving the way she moaned out his name.

"Tell me you're okay, Honey," he begged.

"Yes," she breathed. "Make me yours Texas," she said. That was an order he'd be willing to obey. He watched Jag kiss his way down her body and Tex knew he was waiting for his turn, but there was nothing patient about Jag's demeanor. Tex couldn't blame him. If the tables were turned, he would be clawing at the damn walls, ready to get inside of Remi. She pulled him down and kissed him like a starving woman.

"Let me help you, Jag," she insisted. Jag looked down her body as if he was longing to be exactly where Texas was.

"Alright," he stuttered. Jag stood and let Remi's hands freely roam his body and when she opened her mouth, Jag didn't hesitate to shove his cock in.

"Shit," he hissed. "That feels so good, Baby," Jag said. Watching Remi work Jag's dick in and out of her mouth made him hot. He knew he wouldn't last much longer and he wanted her with him when he came.

"Jag," he begged. "I'm close." He and his friend had taken enough women together that Jag knew exactly what Texas was asking him. He reached down to toy with Remi's nipples and she whimpered around his dick. That seemed to be all poor Jag could take. He shouted her name as he came in spurts down her throat and Remi took all of him, licking his cock clean before letting him pop free from her parted lips.

Texas pumped in and out of her body, loving the way she seemed to fit him perfectly. When Jag sucked her taut nipple into his mouth, Remi wrapped her legs around Tex's ass, tugging him closer. She was so close and Texas knew that her orgasm milking his cock was going to be enough to send him over the edge. Spasms rippled through her body as he pumped into her a few more times, losing himself deep inside of her.

"Fuck," Texas growled. The three of them fell into bed together, Jag on one side of Remi and Texas on the other. They made it a rule to never spend the night with the woman that they shared. It always let to an awkward morning after, but right now, Tex didn't give a fuck. He wanted nothing more than to keep their woman cuddled up between their two bodies all night long.

Remi sighed and shimmied down the bed, standing to find her clothes. "Where the fuck do you think you're going?" Texas asked.

"It's almost one-thirty in the morning and I need to get home," Remi admitted. They didn't really know where Remi lived. All she ever shared with him and Jag was that she lived in NOLA with her sister and that she was originally from New Mexico. Other than that, if he and Jag let her walk out of Reckoning, there was no telling when they might see her again. That thought alone terrified Texas.

"Stay, please," Jag offered. Tex knew that Jag could hear the panic in his voice when he asked where she was going. Hell, he could hear it clear as day, even though he wanted to sound cool and in control—he didn't.

"I can't, Jag. Things get too messy that way. I've helped to change the outcome of my vision, just as I promised and now, it's time for me to go," Remi admitted. Texas hated how cold she sounded about what had just happened between the three of them.

"That's all this was to you, Remi?" Jag asked. Texas stood from the bed and pulled on his jeans. He wasn't about to sit around and watch as Remi so easily walked away from their night together. He'd be the one leaving and if she didn't like that —well, that was too bad.

"We knew the score," Texas drawled. He refused to look at either of them. He knew what he'd find. Jag would be lying in bed confused, sulking, and butt hurt while Remi put her mask firmly back into place. Hell, Texas wasn't sure that she had even removed it to begin with. He wasn't sure if he and Jag had ever met the real Remi; she was always so careful in what she shared with them. Remi never really let them completely in and that really burned his ass.

"Remi warned us that this was just for a night, man. You thought she'd be willing to give us more. Maybe we both were hoping for that, but we were wrong. She doesn't want that from either of us." Texas shot Jag a sympathetic look over his shoulder as he grabbed his cut from the chair and slipped it over his shoulders.

"Texas, please," Remi whispered, touching his arm as he passed to leave.

He coldly shrugged her off. "You did what you came here to do, Sweetheart. You warned Jag and saved his life. I appreciate it, honestly, I do. Mission accomplished, so go on home. There's nothing more for you here, Remi." Texas pushed past her, ignoring the hurt he saw in her eyes. He wasn't a cold-hearted asshole, but he was sure acting like one right now. He didn't give a fuck though. Remi hurt him and all he wanted to do was hurt her right back.

"See you tomorrow night, brother," he shouted over his shoulder to Jag and walked out of their room, not bothering to shut the door. All Texas could think about was getting on his fucking Fat Boy and riding until he didn't give a fuck about how much Remi hurt him. He wanted to ride his bike until the look of disappointment faded from Jag's eyes and Remi's scent disappeared from his own skin, but Tex had a feeling there wouldn't be enough road for that.

# REMI

After Texas all but stormed out of their little room above Reckoning, Remi made one excuse after another to leave, but the hurt and disappointment in Jag's eyes made that impossible for her to do. She ended up staying with him, wanting to give him what he needed but she worried that might be a tall order she'd never be able to fill. Jag had that look in his eyes—the one that told her he was falling for her and Remi couldn't let that happen.

She had been with men—lots of men—both good and bad. Jag and Texas were both good men and the thought of hurting them made her heartache. But, that was what ultimately was going to happen and leaving was her only way out of causing them any more pain. She wasn't the type of woman who did mushy hearts and flowers. She didn't make pretty promises and Lord knows she didn't need any in return. No man had ever given her that—promises, not even Aria's father. He was a huge mistake, another one of the men she got lost in while trying to save his life. He ended up leaving her and who could blame him? He didn't want the baby and when she admitted that she did, he bolted. Remi was pregnant and alone and honestly, happy.

Her grandmother, aunt and sister all helped with Aria and her daughter was the happiest, most beautiful little girl she'd ever known. The memory of her sweet little face and green eyes haunted her nightly dreams. She'd wake from them still able to feel her baby girl's soft curls against her palms and smell her sweet scent. Her daughter always smelled like sunshine and honeysuckle and Remi couldn't get enough of her gentle smiles and devilish laughter. It filled her home and her heart until it was gone; stripped away from her so cruelly, even she didn't see it coming. She should have seen the whole thing—all of them should have, but they were too consumed with seeing others who needed their help. Faceless, nameless others who'd Remi would gladly trade for the chance to have her baby back. It had been just over five years since she had to say goodbye to her baby girl and not a day passed without feeling as though she wouldn't be able to take one more breath without seeing her daughter's face.

Remi had shut out everyone and anything that made her happy. She stopped going out on dates with men who might come to mean more to her than just a casual hook-up. She learned to meet men in dive bars and offer them her body for just one night, taking as much pleasure from them as humanly possible to make it to her next fix. Sex had become that for her —a way to escape her reality and find a way to numb the constant dull ache left from losing her daughter.

Oryana had taken to calling her a "badass", but her twin sister was wrong. What Nena constantly missed was the fear and panic that welled up inside of her every time she saw a baby. It would send her into a spiral that led her back down the dark road of seedy bars and men who just wanted to use her body. Her family had no clue—no one did, not even the one person closest to her. Her twin sister would never understand her need to take what she could from this shit hole of life and find her way forward. It was her only option and one that she never spoke about. Admitting it would mean that she'd have to admit the truth —she had become a monster and most of the time, she didn't even recognize herself anymore.

She spent the night curled up next to Jag's warm body, soaking up the dreams of possibilities that would never be for her. When the sun rose the next morning, she snuck from Jag's bed, found her clothes and left Reckoning. Remi made herself the promise she'd never return to that bar or see the two bikers who spent the night before sharing her body, but she was lying to herself. The idea of seeing both Texas and Jag made her feel like a giddy schoolgirl and she knew that staying away from either of them would be impossible for her. She was a masochist when it came to staying away from things that she wanted; things she knew could tear her heart out. Maybe she liked the pain, who knew. But, Remi would go back to them in a heartbeat if it meant forgetting all the shit life threw at her. Tex and Jag were a nice distraction even though she knew how it all would end between the three of them. It would go down in a shitstorm of fire and by the time she finally got the nerve to leave them, they'd hate her just as much as she already hated herself.

By the time Remi got back to the little house that she shared with Oryana, she found her twin sister already up and having breakfast. Remi walked into the kitchen and tossed her car keys onto the counter, grabbing a coffee mug to pour herself a cup of coffee.

"Long night?" Nena questioned.

"I didn't get much sleep," Remi admitted. It was the truth. Jag had woken her a few times in the night, taking her body as if he needed the constant contact to remind himself that she was still there.

"You okay, Remi?" Nena asked. Her sister wasn't much of a busy body. She usually let Remi do her own thing and didn't ask many questions. It was one of the things she loved most about her twin. But once in a while, Nena seemed to be able to pick up on just how much she was hurting and now was one of those times. She wouldn't lie to her sister, there would be no point in it. Nena could always see through her lies, straight into her soul and that scared the shit out of her. Letting Nena see how dark her soul had become—so filled with hatred and the need for revenge, might just send her sister running as far away as possible. She needed Nena as much as she needed food and air. Her twin sister was part of her—the good part; the light to her darkness.

"Don't ask questions you might not like the answers to, Oryana," Remi warned.

"Geeze, now I'm really worried. You only use my full name when you are pissed. What did I do this time?" Nena teased. That was her sister's way of letting her know that she would back off. She made light of the situation, even joking around with her when Remi had crossed the line and needed to back down.

"You didn't do anything, really. I'm just grumpy from lack of sleep," Remi lied. Nena eyed her as if she didn't believe a word she was saying.

"I just worry about you," Nena admitted. "I know that this time of year is tough for you."

"Don't," Remi ordered. She sounded more like she was begging for her sister not to bring up the topic. Remi knew exactly what time of year it was. They were coming up on the sixth anniversary of her baby's death. Aria would have been eight years old this year, but Remi would never know who her daughter could have become.

"I miss her too," Nena whispered. "We all do, but you have to find a way to go on, Remi. Maybe put yourself out there and go on a date. What about Lyra's friends at her husband's bar?" Nena was hitting a little too close for comfort with her questions and Remi wondered if she had a vision or was just making a really good guess.

"Guys?" Remi questioned, playing dumb.

Nena rolled her hazel eyes at her and smiled. "Yeah—the two guys who helped to find us. What were their names?" From the look on her sister's face, she knew exactly what their names were.

"Texas and Jag," Remi said. "And, I'm not interested."

"Well, they're interested in you," Nena said.

"How exactly would you know that?" Remi asked.

"Tank and Lyra told me that they were sniffing around you. Then, when they found us at the paper factory, you seemed pretty damn happy to see them," Nena taunted.

"Tank and Lyra need to mind their own damn business," Remi grouched, causing her sister to giggle. "And, of course, I was happy to see Tex and Jag," she covered. "They did save our lives." Remi thought back to that dark, musty warehouse where they were kept, against their will. Some government guy named Dave was using them as trackers to find Lyra and her daughter, Delilah. He kept Remi and Nena locked in a make-shift cage, getting as much information as he could about where Lyra might have been hiding.

That was what she and her sister did, found people. They were seers and came from a long line of women who could see things that happened in someone's past or in some cases, future. But Nena and Remi had a special gift of being able to track people. If someone needed help finding a missing person, they could usually see where they were being held or worse, where their bodies had been dumped. She and her twin sister had found countless missing persons over the years and that was one of the reasons they left home. They had become local celebrities back in their small New Mexico town. It had gotten to the point where reporters and people who needed their help, were invading their personal property to talk to them. She and Nena agreed that they couldn't do that to their aunt and grandmother anymore. So, they packed their stuff and left, finding jobs in New Orleans and blending in as much as possible. They went home every chance they got but it wasn't as often as either of them would have liked.

"Anali called this morning," Nena said. "She said that Aunt Joanna isn't feeling well and she wants us to come home. Anali thinks it would be good for our aunt to see us." Remi panicked at the mention of her aunt being sick. When she and Nena were just babies, their mother took off. They really didn't know who their father was, although they had heard the whispered rumors through their small town. They were raised by their Aunt Joanna and their Anali, or grandmother.

Their community was made up of mostly Navajo and most of the people in town were related to each other by either blood or marriage. Everyone knew everyone else's business and she had to admit, at times, she loved her close-knit community. There were also times she wanted to run away and leave her Navajo heritage as far behind her as humanly possible. Now that she was living away from home and her family, Remi missed them more than ever. She and Nena both knew that returning to New Mexico and putting down roots, would never happen for them.

It had only been a little over a year after she lost Aria before things started going haywire around town. She and Nena were involved in a case to find a missing little boy and it hit a little too close to home for Remi. The kid was almost the same age her daughter would have been and she and her sister were able to track him and bring him home to his parents. His babysitter had abducted him after losing her own baby. Remi felt such sadness as she watched the woman being handcuffed and led away as the happy parents were reunited with their child. She realized that she recognized herself in that poor, mixed-up woman and the thought of losing her mind enough to steal someone else's kid scared the living hell out of her. That's when the local press got ahold of the news story and before they knew it people were showing up on Anali's doorstep, demanding that they help find a missing loved one. Their grandmother and aunt convinced them to take off and find a place to make a better life for themselves.

They had, for the most part. Nena was a personal trainer at a local spa and Remi had found a little local library that needed a librarian. It didn't matter that she had no formal schooling or training for the job, they hired her on the spot just because she shared her love of books. They were her way to escape the hellish reality that had become her life and she loved her job. Remi and Nena traveled home to New Mexico every chance they got, but it was never enough. Her grandmother missed them and they missed her.

"Will Aunt Joanna be okay?" Remi asked. Even though she was married and had two daughters of her own, Aunt Joanna always checked in on them both. She helped them go shopping for prom dresses and talked to them about boys and life lessons that might have been hard-learned otherwise.

"Yeah," Oryana said. "They are running some tests but Anali is worried and well, she asked us to come home. We can't say no." Nena was right, they couldn't. Not after everything both women gave up to raise her and her sister. Besides, a trip home might be just what she needed to put the two sexy as sin alphas out of her mind. The only problem would be facing her past demons and being that close to her baby girl's grave. The anniversary of Aria's death wasn't something she was looking forward to.

"Fine," she agreed. "I've got to go into work now, but I'll try to get a few days off at the end of the week." Nena smiled and sipped her coffee, shoving her second donut into her mouth. How her sister ate so much crap and stayed so skinny was beyond her comprehension. It probably had something to do with the fact that Nena worked out every day and had to stay accountable for her clients.

"I'll clear my schedule for the end of the week and maybe we can make it a long weekend trip back home. It will be good to spend time with Anali. I think that Aylen and Kaiah will be home too, visiting their mom. It will be good to see our cousins," Nena said.

"If they are going to be home, why do we need to be there?" Remi grouched. She sounded like a bitch, but she didn't care. Aylen was like a little sister to them. She was the youngest and Remi had to admit, she loved Aylen as if she was her sister and not a cousin. Kaiah, on the other hand, was a class A bitch. She loved to remind her and Nena that they were motherless; something that they knew all too well without their cousin's nasty reminders.

"Because Aunt Joanna asked for us and honestly, I want to see Anali. I know you just had a trip home but it's been almost two months since I've been back and it's time to reconnect and hopefully let some of the bad stuff go. We need to recharge, Remi." Her sister wasn't wrong. After Nena was abducted and kept for over a week, Remi was able to find her in her dreams. Remi went looking for her and she worried she'd never find Nena. Remi had been hiding out from that asshole Dave. Nena was trying to track her down when Dave took her and Remi knew that sooner or later, her connection with her sister might lead her into the same trouble Nena had landed in—so she gave herself up, hoping that together, they would find a way to escape. Dave was looking for a way to pull his own sister out of her coma-like state. Dave's sister was also a seer and she did what she had to do to stay safe from her brother. He wanted to wake her to get the money their parents had left them. His sister, Anna, had basically hidden out in her dream-like world to avoid having to deal with her asshole brother. Anna was smart enough to know that if she woke up, Dave would have gotten his hands on her money and then he'd have no use for her anymore. Anna's brother was a cold-blooded murderer and now he was going to spend the rest of his life in prison for murder and abduction.

When Dave dragged her into that damn cell, to be with Nena, Remi wasn't sure if she wanted to be angry with her sister or throw her arms around Nena and promise that everything would be alright. Nena said that she had hoped her sister had alerted the calvary about where they were, but that hadn't happened—there was no time. Their only way out was to find Lyra and send her clues, through her dreams, as to where they were being held hostage. Lyra and her new husband, Tank were able to follow the clues and they sent Jag and Texas into the old paper factory to find them.

The guys stormed into that damn place, like her knights in shining fucking armor, and she nearly gave in to everything they asked of her then. But, Remi knew better than to believe in all that fairytale nonsense. There was no such thing as a knight in shining armor and if she needed saving, she'd have to do it herself. That was who she was, her own personal savior and that was just fine with her.

## JAG

Jag woke up to an empty bed and the small room that he and Texas rented above Reckoning felt cold and lonely. After Tex stormed out of there the night before, he thought for sure that Remi would be the next to make some lame-ass excuse and leave. But, she didn't. She was dressed and ready to walk out of that room but one word from him, one pleading word changed her mind.

"Stay," he begged and she shut the door, stripped and got back into his bed. He wasn't sure how or why he had gotten so lucky, but he wasn't about to question it. Maybe Remi needed him as much as he seemed to need her. Hell, maybe she was just as lonely and sick of all the bullshit life kept throwing at her. Jag sure was. He could tell that Remi had been through hell and back and it had nothing to do with her being kept in a fucking cage by that asshole, Dave. No, she had lived through her own personal hell and he could see it in her deep, hazel eyes every time she looked at him.

Honestly, Jag knew close to nothing about the dark-haired beauty. She was as mysterious as they came and maybe that's what drew both him and Texas to her. He didn't have much time to lounge around and think about why he needed her as much as he did. Jag had to get back to his place, shower, change and head into work. He had a client paying top dollar to be flown from New Orleans to Miami for the day and he couldn't be late. Besides, flying was just what he needed right now, to take his mind off the crazy night that he and Remi had just spent, tangled up with each other. The only problem was he was going to have to face Texas since they lived together. There would be no dodging his best friend, even if he wanted to.

They needed to get this shit aired out and he wanted answers. Texas owed him an explanation about what the fuck happened last night. Sure, they were both acting like jealous assholes, but it seemed to go deeper with Tex. Once he found out that Remi wasn't submissive, he seemed to check out. Hell, Jag wasn't sure Tex was even going to participate and that just plain pissed him off. They had been waiting for their chance with Remi for months now and his best friend was going to just throw it all away over a little bit of jealousy. The strange thing was that neither of them had ever really had an issue with the green-eyed monster before meeting Remi. She seemed to bring it out in them and if they didn't find a way past it, Jag had a feeling that last night was going to be their one and only night together. He wanted more. He wanted so much fucking more with her and if Tex wouldn't get on board, he'd find a way to convince Remi to give just him a chance.

By the time he got back to the house that he and Tex shared, he had given up all hope of making it into work on time. He called his client and made up some bullshit excuse about lousy weather in Miami and having their flight pushed back by air traffic control. The guy didn't seem too happy, but he bought it and that gave Jag enough time to talk to Texas. Finding his truck in the driveway was just plain dumb luck. Tex was usually an early riser, making his way into work early every day—except this morning.

Jag threw his keys in the bowl by the front door and headed upstairs, to look for Tex. If he wasn't in his room, he knew he'd be able to find him in their home gym down in the basement. Texas was obsessed with working out and given the fact that he had a lot of aggression—both sexual and otherwise to work through, he'd probably be down there.

Jag jogged down to the basement and heard the heavy metal music before he even got to the last step. He turned the corner to find Tex lifting free weights wearing an angry scowl and judging from the amount of sweat pouring off his bare chest, he had been at it for a while now.

Texas slammed down the weights to the basement floor and looked over at Jag, his expression mean. "So, you're finally home?" Tex drawled.

"Yep," Jag said. He crossed the room to face Tex and Jag worried that might have been his first mistake. The guy looked about ready to tear him apart. Jag brazenly turned down the music and Tex huffed out his breath.

"Don't," Tex warned.

"Don't what," Jag asked. "You want to tell me what the fuck that was last night?"

"Not sure what you're talking about, man. We had sex with Remi and I left, that's all." Texas said. He picked up his weights again and cranked back up his music. Jag knew that pushing Tex wasn't the best answer but what choice did he have?

"You just left us there," Jag accused.

"She was on her fucking way out," Texas said. "I'm betting she was hot on my heels after I left and that's what has you all worked up. You didn't get your night of fun and now, you're going to pout like a giant baby and make this somehow be all my fault."

"Nope," Jag said.

"Nope?" Texas questioned. "What the hell does nope mean?"

"It means that Remi didn't take off last night after you left. She stayed." Jag knew he was being an asshole, but he didn't give a fuck. He wanted to hurt Texas just as much as he had been hurt. He just left him hanging and that broke their bro code.

"What the fuck? Remi stayed?" Texas asked.

"Yep, all night," Jag bragged.

"Fuck," Tex swore again and Jag laughed.

"Yeah, a few times, although it's really none of your business. You lost the right to know what happened after you walked out," Jag said.

"How did you get her to stay?" Tex asked, setting the weights back down. He shut off the music and slumped down onto the weight bench. The look of defeat on Tex's face was nearly enough to make Jag feel like a complete ass for rubbing in the fact that he spent the rest of the night with the woman they both wanted.

"I asked nicely," Jag said. He sat down next to Texas on the bench. "Why'd you do it? Why did you leave?" Jag asked.

Texas sighed, "I don't know man. I freaked out when she got out of that bed and started pulling on her damn clothes. All I could think about was how bad I wanted her to stay with me—with us. Hell, I panicked and did all I knew to do, I bolted."

"Yeah, I get that, Tex. But, Remi isn't like other women we've shared. She's different—even special, although I doubt she'll let us tell her that. She's broken man. I know you can see it too, every time she looks at either of us. She's been through something that we might not be able to fix, but God, I want to try to fix her, Tex." Jag chanced a look at his friend and he could tell Tex felt the same way.

"How do we do that if it's not what she wants?" Texas questioned. "You saw her last night, man. She couldn't crawl out from between the two of us fast enough. It was like she was counting down the minutes to be rid of us." Jag knew where Texas was coming from. They had been friends for years now and Jag was pretty sure there wasn't another person on the planet who knew him better. He knew all of Texas' secrets including the dark places of his soul where he didn't believe he'd ever be good enough for anyone else because his own father threw him away, without a second look back.

It was a story that Texas reluctantly told Jag after the first night they shared a woman. The two of them had spent most of that evening, almost five years ago now, drinking and talking. When Texas all but insisted on being his wingman, Jag took him up on his offer. He wasn't much of a lady's man and being home fresh from the terrors of war, made him a little gun shy about putting himself out there. Jag was never very good at talking to women. He'd learn to say just enough to get by, but women seemed to flock to Tex and his good old country boy charm. They couldn't seem to throw themselves at him fast enough and Jag was honestly intrigued by his friend's superhero-like abilities with the opposite sex.

Texas took him under his wing and when the first woman to come along that night nearly jumped at the chance to be between the two of them, Jag almost backed out. But, Texas shot him a look like he'd kill him if he walked away and before he knew it, they were taking the hot little blond up to Texas' room above Reckoning. Sharing women became their thing and after a while, the guys in the club just seemed to accept their wicked ways.

"I don't think that was the case, Tex," Jag offered. "I think she was scared and was doing the only thing she knew to do—run. Honestly, once I asked her to stay, she didn't hesitate."

"Well then, maybe it was just me she couldn't wait to get the fuck away from. Hell, maybe she just wants you and I was a means to an end," Texas said.

"That's the dumbest fucking thing I've ever heard," Jag grumbled. "She wanted both of us and you sitting there sulking isn't going to make any of this mess better. I have a quick flight to Miami, but I'll be home tomorrow morning. How about you get off your ass and go apologize to Remi for acting like a fucking jerk?" Jag waited Tex out, hoping his little speech was enough to give Tex the kick in the ass he needed to make things right with Remi. It was the only way she'd give them the time of day again and Jag needed that—her time. He craved it more than he did his next breath.

Texas nodded, "Fine."

"Thank fuck," Jag growled. He stood and started for the steps. He didn't want to be an asshole, but it was almost like he couldn't stop himself from what he was about to say next. "And Tex," he said, looking back over his shoulder. "Don't fuck it up."

# TEXAS

Texas really didn't have time to sit around and try to figure out his next move with a woman who may or may not want to give him a second chance. Just before Jag left for his flight, he made Texas promise to at least try with Remi. He wasn't sure what his best friend was looking for from him, but he owed it to Jag to at least try. Tex knew that Jag would do at least that much for him if the tables were turned. Right now, he had a job to get to and then, he'd consider his next move with Remi.

By night, he was a badass Reckoning MC member but by day, he was an accountant. Yeah, even he found that fact hilarious. He'd don his business suit, to hide his tats, and head into work to crunch numbers at one of the largest accounting firms in NOLA. Not a lot of people knew what he did for a living. The guys at Reckoning knew since he was in charge of the club's money. He kept tabs on accounts for the MC and for the bar, as Tank's accountant. He also came up with creative, albeit sometimes illegal, ideas for funding the club's various activities. Hedge funds and day trading were his personal favorites and he had to admit, having the club Prez's trust made him feel damn good. Tank wasn't just his friend; he was his brother and Texas was damn thankful for that.

Honestly, he never had friends like the ones he found at Reckoning. They were a band of misfits, made up of guys from all walks of life. Some of them were ex-military, like Jag and even Tank. Others were guys who had done hard time—the club's one-percenters, like him. But, Texas considered every one of them his friend and he was damn lucky to have his club backing him. As a kid, he was bounced from foster home to foster home. It wasn't until he was almost a teen that he found a home that he knew wouldn't toss him back out into the system. Tex was always looking for a family—his place in the world, and that's how he got mixed up with the wrong crowds when he was nineteen and ended up doing time for grand theft auto. While he was in prison, his goal was to keep his head down, serve his time and get out. He served five of his seven years, got out for good behavior and never looked back. He moved from Arizona to New Orleans, looking for a fresh start and that's exactly what he found at Reckoning.

Texas had basically grown up in the foster care system and all things considered, he had it pretty good. His mother died shortly after he was born and his old man had tried to do what he could to raise him, but the alcohol finally won in the tug of war that seemed to play out between him being a decent dad and wanting his next drink. Texas learned at a very young age that he could only count on himself and that was a crappy lesson for any kid. By the time Texas was seven, he had been in three different foster homes and being bounced from place to place was really taking its toll on him. He was hoping to find a family who wanted to keep him, but that had never happened. He found the next best thing though, a foster family who kept him long enough that he could age out of the system and find his own way. The Vasquez family had taken him in when he was ten and he was lucky enough to live with them for the next eight years. They offered to help him out and let him stay after he aged out of the system. He legally changed his last name to Vasquez, pretending to be someone he wasn't. But he knew the score. They needed his bed for another kid and honestly, if he had stayed, he might be keeping another kid from a safe, warm, home. He couldn't do that, so he left. He tried the whole community college thing, but after a few semesters decided that he didn't want to keep spinning his wheels. He ran out of money and when the student loans ran dry, he decided to take drastic measures, joining a gang that would never care about him and doing some pretty dumb shit—like stealing cars.

Tex floundered, trying to find his place, but that never seemed to happen for him. Not until he stumbled into Reckoning one night, to dodge a thunderstorm. He was driving across the country on his bike and he decided to take a break and hopefully find a place to lay low for the night. He found so much more in the little bar that evening. He had met Tank and got into a heated debate over which was more fun to drive, a Harley Sportster or a Softail Classic, with some guy named Jag. Little did he know that he was meeting the two guys who would help shape who he'd become. He owed his entire existence to them.

Tank convinced Tex to finish college and he did, getting his degree in accounting. Tank had floated him the money for tuition and in return, he did Reckoning's books and helped out with the MC portion of things after he was patched in. Jag convinced him to prospect for Reckoning and even agreed to be his sponsor and it finally felt like he had found his home—both in his club and with his friends. Texas had everything he thought he wanted until the leggy, sexy as fuck, brunette walked into Reckoning to warn Tank's ol'lady, Lyra, that she and her daughter were in danger. And now, Remi was all he could think about, day and night and here he went and fucked everything up with her.

****

Texas got off work at six and ran home to shower and change into his jeans, t-shirt, and cut. They had church tonight and he promised Tank he'd be there since Jag was going to be out of town. Jag was Reckoning's new VP and Tank's right-hand man. Texas knew that Tank would need some help with the meeting tonight and besides, the only other thing Tex had on his plate for the evening was to hunt Remi down and find a way to grovel and beg her to give him and Jag another chance.

"You're late," Tank grumbled.

"Sorry, man," Tex said. "Jag and I had a late night and I got to work late this morning." It was mostly true. Jag had a late night with Remi. Texas had fucked up and missed out on possibly that best thing to ever come between him and Jag and ran out of there like a pussy. Texas thought it best to leave that part out since Lyra and Remi were friends.

"What did you do?" Tank growled. Texas shot him a look across the bar. Tank stopped cleaning beer mugs long enough to stare down Tex and his resemblance to an angry grizzly bear didn't have the effect Tank seemed to be hoping for. Tex cracked a smile and Tank sighed, picking up another wet mug to dry. "Fuck," Tank cursed under his breath. "I'm going to have to fucking hear all about your two asses messing shit up from my very pregnant wife, aren't I?"

Yeah, Tank knew exactly what, or in this case who, he and Jag did. Remi met Lyra when she sauntered into Reckoning, claiming to have had a vision that might save Lyra and her daughter Lil's lives. Tank wasted no time whisking his woman and now step-daughter out of town and Texas couldn't blame him. They had all been through a lot of shit together and now, Remi and Lyra were the best of friends.

"Sorry, man," Texas said. "If it helps, I'm betting that it was only for a night and right now, the chances of Remi giving me another shot are slim to none. I don't know how she and Jag left things though."

"Wait." Tank paused from drying mugs again to look at Texas. "You two didn't share her?" Tank knew the score—he and Jag usually shared their women. It wasn't something they hid from their brothers.

"Oh, we shared her," Texas drawled. He knew he was wearing a goofy, shit-eating grin by the way Tank groaned something about him being a "fucking idiot". Texas laughed. "Yeah, that parts true too. I was a fucking idiot, but it has nothing to do with me and Jag sharing Remi."

"Do I want to know what happened, man?" Tank questioned.

Texas shrugged as if it was no big deal, but it was a fucking huge deal. "I got jealous and acted like an ass when she tried to leave last night. I stormed out of the room and well, she spent the rest of the night with Jag." Tank whistled. "Exactly," Texas agreed with Tank's nonverbal assessment. He'd be the first to admit that he royally fucked up with Remi the night before. Tonight though, he planned on making everything right. That was if she'd even give him the chance to explain that he had been a complete ass.

"You gonna fix it?" Tank asked. Hell, he sounded like he was accusing him of something rather than asking a question.

"Yeah," Texas admitted. "Tonight, after church. I just need to find her and well, I have no idea where to even start." He and Jag knew next to nothing about Remi. All they really knew was her name and that she lived somewhere in NOLA with her twin sister, Oryana. New Orleans was a big enough city that someone could get lost in it if they wanted to and he had a feeling that Remi and Nena had good reason to stay lost.

"I may be able to help with that," Tank said. He leaned across the bar like he was about to share a secret and Texas knew better than to compare the big guy to a teenage, gossipy girl. He walked down to the end of the bar and sat on one of the bar stools.

"Shoot," Texas said.

Tank's smile was mean. "You gonna go and fuck things up again, if I tell you where she is?" His tone was light and teasing but Tex could tell that Tank honestly meant his question. If he was being completely honest, his answer would involve the words, "fuck" and "yes" because he was pretty sure that any meeting between him and Remi would end with him fucking up in a big way.

"No," he lied. Tank threw back his head and laughed and Texas sat back on his stool, finding their conversation a whole lot less funny.

"You're such a bad fucking liar," Tank grumbled. "But, you're my brother and well, I need my wife all to myself tonight, if you catch my drift." Tank slammed the clean glass down on the bar and bobbed his eyebrows at Tex, for good measure.

"Yeah, got it man," Texas grouched. "You need to get laid— don't we all? You gonna tell me or not?"

"She's at my house with Lyra, Beth, and Nena, having girl's night," Tank said, making a face. Texas smiled.

"Girl's night?" he asked.

"Yeah and if you can get Remi and Nena out of my house, I'd owe you one," Tank said.

"I'll head over after church," Texas said. "What time are the guys do to get here?" He looked around the mostly empty bar and wondered why no one was there since Tank said he was late for their meeting.

Tank shot him a sheepish grin, "I might have lied to you about the meeting time," he admitted.

"What do you mean?" Texas asked.

"Well, you're late to everything, man. Hell, you're going to be late for your own funeral. Jag told me you were covering for him tonight and we agreed to tell you eight, but the meeting doesn't start til nine." Texas shot him a wolfish grin and hell; he couldn't stay mad at the guy. It was true, he was constantly late. In his hurry to get to the meeting, he had missed dinner.

"Fine," he grumbled. "But, dinner is on you. I'll take two burgers, fries, and a beer." Tanks smile faded and Texas laughed. "Come on man, it's the least you could do for making me rush over here and miss dinner."

"Fine, just as long as you stick to your promise and clear the Nez women out of my house," Tank said. Texas nodded and Tank slid him a beer across the bar. Tex watched as his friend walked back to the kitchen to put in is order, worried that he had just made a promise he wouldn't be able to keep.

# REMI

"Pass the 'passion pink' polish, please," Remi asked Lyra. Her friend handed it over and gasped when their fingers touched. Lyra's gift had certainly intensified since she found out what she was capable of. Remi felt it too, every time her skin came into contact with another seer's—a combination of fire and a flash of vision, either past or present, that was playing through the person's mind at the time of contact. Lyra was thinking about what color to paint the baby's nursery. Apparently, Tank had picked up some paint samples earlier that day, and them having a nail painting party was making her think about her choices. Remi didn't want to even guess what Lyra had seen from their quick contact. She had been playing her night with Jag and Tex on a loop in her mind and if Lyra's surprised gasp was any indication, that was exactly what she had seen.

"So," Remi asked, wanting to change the topic before it was even brought up. "Have you guys decided on if you want to find out if the baby is a boy or a girl?" She knew that Lyra probably had some inclination, but her friend had stubbornly kept it to herself, not even telling Tank. He insisted that he wanted to be surprised, but Tank didn't strike Remi as the type who liked surprises.

"No," Lyra said.

"I already know," Beth chimed in. As a seer, Beth probably knew a lot of things that she had to keep bottled up to herself. "I'm having a boy," Beth said, rubbing her belly. "And, Lyra is having a—" Lyra covered Beth's mouth, careful not to smear her polished wet nails.

"Shut the hell up, Beth," Lyra shouted. "I told you not to tell anyone." Beth giggled and Lyra slowly removed her hand and checked her nails.

"If it makes you feel any better," Nena said. "I already know." Lyra's eyes widened and Oryana giggled. "I won't tell Tank, promise," she said, crossing her heart for good measure.

"Do you know too?" Lyra asked Remi. She smiled and nodded.

"Sorry," she offered. "I think you should probably choose the second blue you were thinking of, for the nursery." Lyra's smile lit up the room and her eyes filled with tears. Sadness filled Remi's heart at how happy Lyra and Beth seemed about their babies. She remembered feeling that way when she was pregnant with Aria, but now wasn't the time or place to drudge up those memories. She had never shared with anyone about her daughter except her family. Nena shot her a sympathetic look and she shook her head. Not now, Nena. Remi thought. She knew that sooner or later, she would have to share with her new friends about her daughter's death, but now wasn't that time. She'd never do anything to upset Lyra or Beth, they were too important to her.

"He's going to look just like Tank," Beth mock whispered.

Lyra rolled her eyes and giggled. "I just hope he doesn't come out as big as Tank." She crossed her eyes and they all giggled.

"It doesn't work that way," Beth chided. "Since you're the only woman in the room to have given birth, you should already know that." Remi's heart sank and when Nena opened her mouth as if she wanted to correct Beth, she sent her sister another pleading look.

Remi stood and put the cap on the pink nail polish she was using. "I promised my friend that I'd look in on her cat while she's away. I better get over there before it gets too late," Remi lied.

"You want me to come with?" Nena asked. "I don't mind."

"No," Remi said. "You should stay here and have fun. I'm just tired and a little grumpy. Getting home and hitting the sheets might be best for me. Can you find a ride home?" She left out the part where she wished she was hitting the sheets with the two hot, sexy bikers she was with last night, but that information wasn't something she was ready to share with Beth or Lyra.

"Reaper and I can drop her home," Beth offered.

"Okay," Nena said. "I'll see you later, Sissy." Oryana shot Remi a concerned look and she plastered on her best fake smile, trying to put her sister at ease. She hugged Beth and Lyra goodbye and ducked her head into the family room, where Lyra's six-year-old, Delilah, was watching TV and said goodbye. Lil smiled and waved, barely taking her eyes from her show. Remi giggled and grabbed her jacket and bag, slipping on her shoes to head out. She opened the front door and ran into what felt like a brick wall. Remi stumbled backward to try to catch her balance.

"Tex," she whispered, looking up at the big guy who posed as a barrier, keeping her from leaving Lyra's house. He reached out and wrapped his arms around her body, trying to help steady her.

"Sorry," he grumbled.

"Not a problem. I should have been watching where I was walking," Remi covered. "Excuse me." She tried to sidestep the big guy and he moved to block her path.

"Actually," Tex whispered, clearing his throat. "I need to talk to you, please," he added and smiled down at her. Remi thought she was only inwardly groaning, but apparently, she was wrong. It ripped from her chest and Texas took a step back from her as if she'd actually slapped him.

Remi instantly felt bad for her reaction to him. "I'm sorry, Tex. It's just been a damn long day and I want to go home and crawl into bed." She didn't miss the way his eyes flashed when she mentioned the crawling into bed part.

He didn't make a move or a peep and the way he watched her made Remi so damn hot. He was waiting for her agreement and Remi felt as if her girl parts were turning into molten lava.

"Texas," she said, leaning into his big body.

He took a step towards her. "Yeah," he whispered back.

"This is a really bad idea," she said.

"I just want to talk," he murmured, his warm breath felt like a caress on her cheek and before she knew what was happening or why, she was nodding her agreement.

"Let me just give my sister a heads up. Can you drop me at my house?" she asked. Texas didn't hesitate his agreement.

"Wait here," she ordered. Remi left Tex standing in the open front door and walked back to the kitchen to find Nena giggling with Beth and Lyra. God, she didn't want them to make a bigger deal out of her going with Texas than was needed, but she knew the girls well enough to know that wasn't going to happen.

"Um," she squeaked, interrupting their laughter.

"Hey—you change your mind about leaving?" Nena asked.

"No," Remi breathed. "I just wanted to let you know that you can have the car. I have another way home." Remi tossed the keys onto the kitchen counter, across from where Nena was sitting and turned to quickly leave. She was hoping to get out of there without any questions.

"How?" Beth called. Remi turned back to face the three of them, all eyes on her.

"Sorry?" Remi asked, pretending not to follow. She knew exactly what her friend was asking.

"How are you getting home?" Lyra asked. Nena looked around Remi and the other women's eyes followed. Before he even said anything, she knew exactly what or in this case who, they were looking at.

"Hey Tex," Lyra said. "You know that Tank's down at the bar. Did you miss church?"

"Lyra, ladies," he drawled. Remi rolled her eyes at the way her three friends seemed to collectively swoon at the big lug. "No, I made it in time for church and then came here to talk to Remi."

"Why do you need to talk to my sister?" Nena questioned, blowing on her wet nails.

"Shit," Remi grumbled. Nena knew exactly who she spent the night with last night and from the smirk on her sister's face, she wasn't going to just let Texas off the hook. Nena liked to toy with people—especially big, hunky, tattooed bikers."

"Um, just some stuff I need to clear up," he offered.

"I thought you were going to wait by the door," Remi whispered.

"And, I thought I was pretty clear last night when I explained that I don't take orders—from anyone." Texas looked her over as if waiting for her to challenge him and she sighed, knowing that if they got into it now, her friends would all know that she slept with him. Some things were private—namely the men she chose to have sex with. Remi knew that sooner or later her easy-going stance on sex would catch up with her and it looked like she was about to have her first collision with reality.

"Fine," she breathed, turning back to face her nosey sister and friends. "I fucked Tex and Jag last night and Tex, here acted like an ass. I'm assuming he came to apologize and now, I'm rethinking actually going with him." There, all out in the open where they can dissect it and talk about it all they'd like. Because despite what she just said, there was no way she was going to miss out on hearing the big guy grovel and beg her forgiveness. She was going to go with him, listen to his apology and then let him down easy. Because falling into bed with Texas or Jag again couldn't happen. It would be too real for her then and Remi didn't do real anymore.

"Well, there you have it," Texas said. "You coming or not, Remi?" he asked. God, she didn't want to be the girl who followed the guy around like a fucking puppy dog, but here she was, agreeing to do just that.

"Yes," she spat. Nena barked out her laugh and Remi shot her a look that had her laughing even louder.

"See you in the morning, Sissy," Nena called after her. She could hear the three of them giggling like loons as Tex grabbed her bag for her, holding the door. Remi was sure he was just making sure she would follow through with her promise, but he should have learned that she never reneged on her promises, from their night together.

"After you," he said.

"Yeah, yeah," Remi grumbled. She walked over to Tex's pick-up truck and looked back at him. "I thought you rode a bike?" she asked.

Texas' smile was easy, "I do but I doubled back home after church and picked up my truck. I didn't know how you'd feel about riding on my bike." Remi hopped into the passenger seat when he opened the door for her. She was trying to ignore her stupid heart for feeling like it skipped a beat at the mention of him thinking about her or considering her feelings at all. That's not what this was about. She was going to hear Tex out and let him down easy—nothing else. The last thing Remi wanted was to lose her new friends and since they were tied to Reckoning, she had to tread carefully.

"I appreciate that, Tex. For the record, I love to ride on motorcycles," she lied. Remi had never been on the back of a bike in her life. But, none of that mattered. She didn't plan on getting on the back of Texas', so why give him the truth. He laughed and shook his head as if he didn't believe her.

"I'm not sure what the game is here, Honey," he said. "But, I'll play."

"What do you mean by game?" Remi asked. Yeah, she was totally playing with him, but admitting to that would never happen. "So, where are you taking me to talk, Texas?"

"My place?" he sounded more like he was asking her than telling her.

"That's not a good idea," she warned.

"Why not?" he asked.

"I think we have two different ideas of what's going to happen tonight, Texas," Remi challenged. "I agreed to talk to you, but that's it."

"Alright," he said. "How about we go back to Reckoning and that way there's no pressure. We can have a few beers and talk."

Remi barked out her laugh, "Because last night worked out so well. Are you just going to pretend that you and Jag don't have a room above the bar? Is this part of the plan? What—Jag's waiting at Reckoning and you two are planning a repeat performance?"

Texas smiled, "Naw. You know all too well about the room, but Jag's not going to be there tonight. He's out of town on business. Sorry to disappoint you but it's just you and me tonight." Why Texas would think that being alone with him was a disappointment was crazy. There was nothing disappointing about the man and the thought of being completely alone with Texas made her a little hot. Remi needed to get her stupid hormones under control and remember her damn rule of one night, one-time deal. Otherwise, she was going to fall for two guys who could possibly tear down her walls and she wouldn't let that happen.

"Fine, Reckoning it is," she reluctantly agreed. Tex had them there in just a few minutes and pulled into the bar. Lyra and Tank's new house wasn't far from there and Remi found herself suddenly wishing she had more time to prepare herself for having to deal with Tex. Jag was the more laid back of the two and the way Tex watched her, so intensely, she worried that he'd be able to see through her defenses and that scared the crap out of her. Remi was always careful to keep her walls in place because she knew that one slip could have her whole life crumbling around her.

Tex parked his pick-up in the dark, back corner of the lot and cut the engine. "I'm sorry, Remi," he almost whispered.

"Wow—you're just going to jump right in, aren't you?" she teased

"I never meant to hurt you last night. I acted like an ass," he admitted.

"Yeah, you did," she agreed.

"You don't have to be so quick to agree, Remi," he grouched. "Give me another chance."

Remi sighed. "You know I can't do that, Tex. You guys were fun for the night but that's where this all ends."

"Why?" he questioned. "Why does it have to be limited to just a night?"

Texas turned to face her but made no move to touch her. Remi was thankful for that because if he had, she would have let him, and they'd probably end up in his room again. The only difference was she wouldn't have Jag there to run interference for her and Tex would ask her for too much. Remi had a feeling he would demand everything from her and she wasn't sure she was ready to give him or anyone that part of her.

"There are things about me that you don't know. If you did, you wouldn't be asking me for another chance, Tex." Remi looked out her window, wishing she was anywhere else but in the parking lot at Reckoning.

"I don't care about all of that," he promised. "Come home with me. Talk to me," Tex asked. Remi knew she should have said no, but when she opened her mouth to speak, she agreed. She fucking agreed.

# TEXAS

Texas wasn't taking any chances that Remi would change her mind. He practically ran every light and blew most of the stop signs between Reckoning and his house. Once Remi gave him her agreement, he couldn't seem to get home quick enough. He knew she might not be agreeing to everything his dick was hoping she was, but she had agreed to hear him out and hopefully give him a chance. That was more than he expected when he showed up at Tank's place tonight. Hell, he expected her to tell him to get lost, but she didn't. She even admitted to her friends and sister that they had slept together. Now, he just needed for her to agree to give him and Jag another chance or his best friend was going to beat his ass when he got home. He promised Jag he'd try and if his unruly cock had his way, he'd do more than just try with Remi tonight.

He parked his truck in the third garage bay and shut the door. "You sure about this, Remi?" he asked. He didn't want to even ask her that, but he also wanted to give her one final chance to back out.

"I—I think so," she stuttered. "Just talking though," she said. She honestly looked scared to death and he wanted to pull her onto his lap and tell her that everything was going to be alright. How could he make her that promise without knowing what had her spooked?

"Sure," he said. "How about you let me make you something to eat?" he asked.

"I'm good," she lied.

"Well, I'm starving and I'm thinking grilled cheese," he said. She smiled at him and nearly took his breath away.

"Nena and I love grilled cheese sandwiches," she admitted. "My Anali used to make them for me."

"Anali?" he questioned.

"Yes," she said. "It means grandmother in Navajo."

"How about we go on in and I'll make us some grilled cheese and you can tell me about your grandmother," Tex offered. He felt like he was holding his damn breath hoping that she'd agree.

"Sure," she said. He got out of his truck and led the way into his kitchen, careful not to touch Remi. If he did, he'd do exactly what he had been thinking about doing since finding her standing in Tank's doorway. He wanted to make her his and prove that they were good together, no matter who was in charge but hell, he wanted her to give him what he needed from her—namely, her submission.

Remi settled onto a bar stool that they kept by the center island and Texas had to admit she looked damn good in their space. "Something to drink?" he asked.

"Um, sure—whatever you have," Remi said. He pulled a couple beers out of the fridge and everything he needed to make sandwiches. He got to work, loving the way Remi watched him. It was nice to have her full attention and honestly, it wouldn't be a bad idea for them to spend some one-on-one time with her if this thing between the three of them was going to work.

"Tell me about your grandmother—what did you call her again?" Tex asked.

"Anali," Remi said. "She raised Oryana and me after our mom took off."

"How old were you?" Texas asked.

"Um." Remi smiled.

"If I'm prying, just say the word. I'm just trying to get to know you a little Remi," Texas admitted.

"I'm not used to talking about myself this much," she said.

"What do you usually talk about when you're, you know—on a date?"

"I don't," she said, taking a swig of her beer.

"You don't talk?" he questioned. Texas flipped the sandwiches and turned off the burner, giving Remi his full attention.

"No, I don't go on dates," she said. She looked down at her beer bottle, fixated with peeling the sticker off as if trying to avoid eye contact.

"Look at me, Remi," he ordered. He didn't expect her to concede, but when she did, it felt as if his whole world turned right side up. "What do you mean by you don't go on dates?"

Remi sighed and looked him dead in the eyes as if accepting his challenge. "I don't go on dates, Tex. I meet guys in bars, hook-up and we fuck." His smile was easy although he felt anything but. The thought of Remi meeting up with random guys at the bar and agreeing to go home with them to have sex, had him seeing red.

"Fuck," he swore. "You aren't kidding?"

"Nope," she admitted. "So, now you know one of my deepest, darkest secrets. Ready to take me home, Tex?" she asked. He was far from ready to take Remi home, but she seemed determined to push him as far away, as quickly as possible.

"How about we eat first and then, if you want me to, I'll run you home after?" he asked.

Remi shrugged and sat back down on her stool. "Suit yourself," she said. Texas passed her the plate with her sandwich and she scarfed it down. He barely touched the two grilled cheeses he made for himself, passing her another sandwich from his plate.

Remi looked up at him like he lost his mind. "I had two burgers at Reckoning. I guess I wasn't as hungry as I thought," he lied. Tex watched her as she polished off his sandwich and handed him back her empty plate.

"Thanks," she said.

"Why don't you date?" he asked. He sounded like a dog with a fucking bone, questioning her the way he was, but he didn't care. He had to know.

"It's just easier that way," Remi said. "I don't do attachments and I can still blow off some steam." He wanted to laugh at the fact that what she was saying sounded like something he or Jag would have said. Except hearing those words come out of Remi's mouth sounded a whole lot less funny to him.

"Is that why you like to be in charge?" Tex asked.

"I don't know if it's a matter of being in charge, but I like to feel like I'm the one in control." Remi gave him her honesty. "I've had so much happen in my life," her voice cracked and he wondered if she would stop talking, but she continued to tell him her story. He rounded the kitchen island and pulled her into his arms, lifting her as if she weighed nothing. "Wait—" Remi protested, "where are you taking me?"

"Just to the sofa. I want to hold you—nothing else," Tex said. Remi looked as if she might protest, but Tex held her tightly against his body and damn if she didn't feel right in his arms. "Go on," he prompted, settling on the sofa with Remi snuggled onto his lap. He could tell that her rebellious nature had kicked in and she looked like she wanted to tell him to let her up.

He felt as if he knew exactly where she was coming from, and Tex wanted for her to tell him everything—all of it, every ugly detail.

"Please, Remi. I just want to know you—all of you. Tell me you want to give this thing between us a chance," he begged. He didn't care if he sounded like a lunatic. He just wanted his chance with her. He promised Jag that he'd make things right with her and originally, he was doing it for his best friend. But now, he knew the truth. He was really trying to convince Remi to give them another chance for himself.

Texas wondered how far she'd let him push her before she told him to take her home. He worried that if he told her his story—the whole thing, she'd never want to see him again. And then there was the jealousy issue that he and Jag needed to work out if they were going to find a way forward. He had never been jealous of anyone in his life but watching Jag with Remi made him madder than hell. Knowing that she spent the rest of the night with Jag after he stormed out of their room above Reckoning pissed him off.

He just couldn't shake the feeling that Remi wanted Jag more than she did him and he had to know. "Do you want Jag more than me?" he asked.

"What—no," Remi protested. "Why would you asked me something like that?"

"I don't know. I'm being a jealous asshole, maybe. But, I see the way you look at him. You don't look at me that way, Remi." Yeah, now he knew he sounded like a jealous asshole. Saying it out loud only drove that point home for him.

"No, Texas," she whispered. "You are two very different people and I want both you and Jag. I look at you both the same." He smiled and nodded but he didn't believe a word of what she was saying.

"You don't believe me, do you?" she asked.

"No," he breathed. "But, that is more my fault. I don't trust very easily and well, I have issues, you might say."

"Don't we all," Remi breathed.

"Yeah—tell me," he demanded. "Tell me everything, Remi. I'm not going anywhere, just give me a chance." Remi barked out her laugh and he was sure that was going to be the end of their conversation. Disappointed didn't even begin to cover how Tex was feeling, but then again, he should be used to it.

## REMI

Remi reached up and cupped Texas' jaw, loving how his beard prickled her skin. His dark hair and eyes were so familiar to her that every time he looked at her, it felt like she was home. "You've been through as much as I have, haven't you, Texas?" she asked. She could feel it, deep down inside of her, she knew that Texas had a story that would parallel hers.

"Yes," he whispered, leaning into her touch.

"I can see it in your eyes," she said. "We're so much alike."

Tex smiled, "Is this part of the seer thing?" She shrugged, not quite sure what this was.

"It's not how I normally do things, but possibly. The first time I ever met you and Jag, you seemed familiar to me. I thought that maybe I had seen you in a vision—I don't know, it all seems crazy now. It's like we know each other, even though we just met."

"I feel the same way," he admitted. Tex stroked back a strand of her long hair from her face and she thought it was the sweetest, gentlest gesture. Texas was big and almost menacing looking. She knew from experience he could hold his own in a fight. When they stormed into that paper factory, to rescue her and Nena, he and Jag fought off the guards like they were nothing. He was a badass, motorcycle riding, hot as fuck, man and Remi had no idea what to do with him or the crazy feelings that were coursing through her body every time he so much as touched her. As if reading her mind, Tex leaned in to gently kiss her lips. He broke their quick kiss and looked so serious she could almost feel his sadness.

"My mom died just after I was born and my old man decided he liked the bottle better than me," Texas whispered.

"Oh, Tex," Remi soothed. Before she could get another word out, he covered her mouth with his big hand.

"Let me just get it out," he barked. "I was put into foster care when I was just a kid. Really, it wasn't that bad. But, I learned at an early age that I'm expendable. I guess that's why I crave control as I do and why I freaked out last night." Hearing Tex lay it all out for her tugged at her heart. She thought he was just being an asshole last night when she refused to let him have her control. They were so much alike in that aspect. "I'm guessing it's the same for you?" he asked.

Remi nodded, "Yeah," she breathed. "My mother took off when Nena and I were little, and we never knew who our father was. Our grandmother and Aunt Joanna raised us. It wasn't bad, really but when people found out what Nena and I could do, things got crazy. They were showing up on our doorstep, asking for us to find people for them and we didn't want to put Anali through that. So, we left New Mexico and landed here."

"I'm from Arizona. You miss the desert?" he asked. She did, so much.

"Yes, but this is our home now. I work down at the library, in town and Nena is a personal trainer." She felt herself make a face when she said that and Texas laughed.

"Not into the whole fitness thing?" he teased.

"Not like Oryana," Remi admitted. "She works out twenty-four seven and can eat whatever she wants. She's so perfect; makes it hard to be around her sometimes."

"Sure," Texas said, palming her ass. "Oh, I think you're pretty damn near perfect yourself, Remi." Hearing him say that was nice, but she felt far from perfect. He couldn't see what she was hiding on the inside. She was messy and ugly—far from perfection. Remi had become a monster, devoid of all human emotions. She hadn't let herself feel anything for anyone in so long, she worried that letting Texas in now was a mistake. He was so easy to talk to; she craved his connection.

"Thanks, but you don't know me," she whispered.

"I'd like to," he said back. "How about if I tell you mine and you tell me yours?"

"What—no," she almost shouted. "I—I can't. You won't like the person I am on the inside, Tex," she warned.

"Try me," he said. "Just give me a chance." God, he sounded like he was begging her and that was the last thing she wanted. She was nothing for him to beg for and once she said the words; once they were out of her mouth, he'd feel the same way about her.

"I'll go first," he whispered. "I served five years in an Arizona state prison for grand theft auto." Remi didn't hide her surprise; her gasp was a dead giveaway that she had no clue.

"You are a criminal?" she asked.

Texas rolled his eyes and smiled. "I was a criminal. I did the crime and served my time. I got mixed up with the wrong crowd and before I knew it, I was doing dumb shit, like stealing cars."

"Yeah, that qualifies as dumb shit," she agreed. Texas chuckled and tugged her against his body.

"You think any worse of me, Honey?" he asked. "You want to run for the door and never look back?" Remi thought his question over and honestly, she didn't His past was just that, past.

"I'll reserve judgment, for now," she teased. "How did you break free from that life after you got out?"

"Well, I didn't at first. I was working odd jobs, back in Arizona because no one wanted to hire a felon. Hell, I was spinning my wheels and going nowhere fast. I had a few semesters at a community college under my belt, before I went to prison. I really wanted to go back to school but I had no money and no bank was going to give me a loan. So, I left Arizona. I got on my bike and just rode. I stayed in a town long enough to make some money to get me to the next town and eventually, I ended up in NOLA at Tank's bar. We got to talking and he introduced me to Jag—the rest is history. Tank gave me a job, tending bar at Reckoning and I patched into the club. He even lent me the money to go back to college, to get my CPA."

"Wait," Remi sat up on his lap. "You're an accountant?" He nodded his head and she laughed. The idea of the badass biker, putting on a suit and going to work to crunch numbers, was almost too much.

"Gee, thanks for that, Honey," Tex grumbled.

"Well, look at you," she sounded like she was accusing him of something. "You don't really look like the kind of guy who works in an office." She looked Tex's body up and down, taking in every delicious inch of him and when she finally worked her way up to his gorgeous brown eyes, she realized he was doing the same to her.

"Tex," she warned, holding up her hands, pressing them into his massive chest. She could feel his heat through his black t-shirt and quickly pulled her hands back, not trusting her own judgment when it came to the sexy biker.

"Your turn," he said. Remi blinked up at him, trying to figure out what the hell he was talking about.

"My turn?" she asked.

"Yep—to share," he reminded. God, the last thing she wanted to do was share the details from her sordid past. She could see right through the game Texas was playing. He was giving her an ultimatum—sex or the truth about her ugly past. Well, she'd give him his truth and then she'd walk away because there was no way he'd want to keep her then.

"I killed my daughter," she whispered. She wasn't sure he had even heard her until she looked up into his eyes, to see the shock and terror she felt every day of her life.

"Come again," Tex said.

Remi sighed. She tried to stand up from his lap, but Tex wouldn't allow it. He banded his arms around her waist and held her against his body. Fine, if he wanted to do it this way, she'd give him the whole ugly, messy truth while staring him down.

It had become so familiar to her—the grief and sadness that consumed her daily, she could tell the story without shedding a single tear. For the first few years, she didn't even speak about her daughter. When she started to finally talk about Aria, she realized just what kind of person she had truly become. She was dead on the inside; incapable of emotions or feelings. She had become the monster her mind told her she was and now, Remi could recount the entire ordeal without any messy emotions getting in the way.

"Aria was only two," she said. "I should have seen it, but I didn't. Hell, do you know how many countless people I saved over the years, seeing their fate before it happened and helping them to change it?"

"Like you did for Jag, last night?" Tex asked.

"Yes," she hissed. "You would think that would win me some kindness from the fucking universe," she shouted to the ceiling as if trying to let the whole world hear her. But, as usual, the universe didn't give a shit about her. "Instead, I put my baby into her car seat and didn't even see that drunk driver coming. My car flipped three times and she was gone before the EMT's even showed up to the scene."

Texas squeezed her tighter and she was sure he was going to squeeze the life out of her. "I'm so sorry, Baby," he murmured. "It's not your fault though."

"It's totally my fucking fault," Remi shouted. "I should have seen that guy coming. I should have fucking known that Aria's life was going to end. I could have changed the outcome. I should have never put her in her seat and gone out that night. She was supposed to be asleep in her crib, but I forgot to get milk for the next morning and I knew she'd be up at dawn, wanting her breakfast. So, I woke her and bundled her up, put her in her car seat. We just never made it to the store and my daughter never saw another morning."

"She's the reason why you want to control everything in your life," Texas said. "You lost control when Aria died and now, you need it at all times."

Remi had never thought about it like that before, but Tex was right. "Yes," she said. "Control and trust go hand in hand for me and I don't trust anyone. Sometimes not even myself." How could she trust anyone? People were always disappointing her and trusting herself would mean that she forgave herself for Aria's death and that would never happen.

"That's why this thing between us won't ever work. You need control as much as I do, Tex." The thought of finally breaking down and telling someone about what happened to her and now, having to walk away from him, broke her. She had taken a leap of faith only to have every small glimmer of hope she was feeling, dashed.

"Now wait just a damn minute," Tex growled. "You're not even going to try."

"No." she stood from his lap and immediately wanted to take back her words after seeing the disappointment on Tex's face. "Don't make this any harder than it needs to be, Texas," she begged. He pulled her back down on his lap and rolled her under his big body, effectively trapping her between him and the sofa.

"How about a compromise?" he asked. Remi could feel his erection pressing against her thigh and it was taking all of her will power not to grind herself against him.

"What type of compromise?" she breathed. Her voice sounded needy and breathless as if she had just run a damn race. Texas smiled down at her like he knew exactly what he was doing to her.

"How about we find a way to both be in control. I'll tell you what I want and you tell me what you want and we'll find a way to meet in the middle—compromise," he said.

Remi giggled, "I do know what compromise means, Tex. I'm a librarian," she reminded him.

"Yeah, I caught that, Honey. I have to say that the idea of you telling me to be quiet while looking at me over your glasses, makes me hot."

"Um," she squeaked. "I don't wear glasses."

"You know what I'm getting at," Tex growled. "The whole hot librarian thing works for me." Remi smiled up at him, letting all the dirty things she could think of doing to him in a library, run through her mind. "Yeah, now you're getting it, Honey. Tell me you'll give this a shot."

"What about Jag?" she questioned. Tex's smile faded.

"If you don't want to do this without him, I understand," he said. Tex rolled off her body and she instantly missed his weight. He had just told her that he worried she didn't want him as much as she did Jag and now, she went and stuck her foot in her mouth.

"That's not what I meant, Tex," she covered. He sat down next to her on the sofa and Remi knew if she didn't do something to convince Tex that she wanted him, he might just take her up on her offer to end their evening and take her home.

Remi crawled onto his lap, straddling his erection between them. "Does this feel like I don't want you, Tex?" she asked, shamelessly rubbing herself against his cock. They were both fully clothed, but she could feel the heat radiating off Tex's big body. He wanted her just as much as she wanted him.

"No," he stuttered. She loved that she had the power to make Tex stutter.

"How about this?" she asked, kissing a path down his neck and gently sinking her teeth into his shoulder. "Does that feel like I don't want you, Texas?"

"Fuck," he swore. "No," he agreed.

"What do you want me to do to you, Tex?" she questioned. Remi liked the idea of the two of them working out their power struggle by each giving and taking what they wanted and needed from each other.

"Take off your shirt," he hissed. "I want to see you, Remi." She smiled and eagerly pulled her shirt up her body and over her head, tossing it to the floor.

"Done," she said. "But, that wasn't much of a compromise, since I wanted us both to be naked, as soon as humanly possible. Now, it's your turn. Shirt please," she said, holding out her hand.

Tex smiled, "With pleasure," he teased. She watched as he yanked his black t-shirt up over his muscles, revealing his tattoos and all Remi could think about was tracing his tats with her tongue. She wanted to taste him all over.

"I love the way you're looking at me right now, Baby," he said. Remi had to admit, she liked looking at him and every time he praised her, she felt a little giddy with joy from hearing that she pleased him. It was almost as if her inner goddess had roared to life and she was a needy bitch who soaked up every ounce of praise she was given.

"Pants too?" she asked.

"You first," Tex countered. Remi stood and shimmied out of her leggings, standing completely bare except her lacy thong and bra. Tex's eyes roamed her body and he pulled her back down to kiss her.

"Pants," she mumbled against his lips.

"Bossy," he teased

"Compromise," she reminded. He chuckled and stood her up from his lap. Tex stood and shucked out of his jeans and God, the man was beautiful. He stood gloriously naked in front of her and it took all of her will power not to push him down to the sofa and sink down over his cock.

"No underwear?" Remi asked.

"Nope," he admitted. "I really don't care for them."

"Well, thank God for that," she teased.

"In fact, I think you should lose yours. You know—even the playing field," he said. Remi slowly pulled her lacy panties down her long legs, putting on quite the show for Texas. She knew exactly what she was doing to him and judging by his erection jutting out at her, she was doing it right. Texas seemed to grow more and more impatient by the moment and when she casually reached for her bra, he reached around her body and helped her out.

"Geeze, Texas," she chided. "You seem to be in a hurry."

"I am," he agreed. "I need to be balls deep inside of you, as soon as possible. I don't have time for the sexy little show you were putting on to torture me, Baby." Remi bit back her moan at his confession of wanting to be balls deep inside of her. She could think of nothing else she wanted more.

"Yes, please," she groaned, pushing Texas back down to the sofa. Remi slowly lowered her wet core over his cock and when she was completely seated, he stilled inside of her, tugging her body against his own. Remi watched Texas as if waiting for him to make the next move. He was so gentle with her and when he reached up to frame her face with his big hands, it was almost too much.

"Spend the night with me," he asked.

"The whole night?" she questioned.

"Yes. Give me what you gave Jag last night. Give me what I was too stupid to realize I wanted or needed. I shouldn't have walked out of Reckoning, Baby. I was an ass. Forgive me?" They sat like that, joined in the most intimate way, him waiting her out for an answer.

"Yes," she breathed. "And, yes." Texas smile nearly lit up the entire room.

"You forgive me?" he questioned.

"Yep and I'll stay the night here with you, Texas."

"I think we're getting to be pretty fucking good at this compromise thing, Honey," Tex teased. "What's your next order?" he asked.

"Move, Tex. Make me yours," she begged.

"Your wish is my command," he whispered and rolled her body underneath his, pinning her to the sofa again. Yeah, they were getting damn good at compromising—especially compromising positions.

# JAG

Jag was exhausted by the time he pulled into his garage. It was just about midnight and all he wanted to do was crawl into his bed and catch up on the sleep that he gave up having to deal with his overly demanding client. They had gotten back to New Orleans about twelve hours ahead of schedule since the guy's meeting had been canceled. He had to listen to his client drone on about the business world for most of their trip and he had to admit, he was looking forward to a little quiet time.

He grabbed a glass of water from the kitchen and was about to head up to his room when he heard what he believed to be a woman's moaning coming from Tex's room. It had been a damn long time since either of them had taken a woman without the other and Jag wondered what the hell was going on. When he left, earlier that morning, Tex had promised to find Remi and apologize and now, he was fucking some woman in his room?

Jag made as much noise as possible as he made his way down the hallway to Texas' room. How could he do this to him? How could he finally take the woman they had both wanted for so long now and throw away all their chances twenty-four hours later? Remi was more than just a piece of ass for Jag and if she wasn't enough for Tex, they could just go their separate ways. Tex would always be his best friend, but he wouldn't give up Remi.

"Don't stop, Baby," he heard Texas beg. Jag turned the corner and walked right into Texas' room with no fanfare. He wasn't about to make some big announcement that he was in the room or God forbid, ask forgiveness for being there.

He saw two shadows, the woman was on top of Tex, riding him and from the way they were both moaning, they were both close to finishing. "Fuck," Jag cursed when he realized the woman was Remi. He wasn't sure if he felt relieved or completely pissed off, finding them in bed together. Their moans grew louder and Jag sat down on the edge of the bed.

"What the fuck," Texas grumbled, looking down at Jag. "What are you doing here, Jag?"

"I take it Remi accepted your apology?" She smiled at Jag and rolled off Texas' body. "Oh, don't let me stop your fun, Honey," he said. Jag knew he sounded like an asshole, but he really didn't care.

"What was the plan here guys? You fuck each other while I'm not home and then what? Tomorrow, when I was supposed to get home, you'd let me down easy—tell me to get lost?" Texas moaned and got out of bed, finding a pair of sweatpants to slip on.

"No one was going to let you down easy," he mumbled.

"Then, what was the plan, Tex? Were you going to rub it in that you got the girl and I'm out?"

Remi crawled down the bed to him, wearing nothing but her smile, and he nearly swallowed his damn tongue. "He's not getting the girl," she said. She didn't hesitate, just crawled up onto his lap to straddle him.

"What the fuck does that mean?" Texas spat. "I thought we worked all that out." Remi reached behind her body, holding out her hand for Tex to take. He did and she pulled him down to sit next to Jag.

"First of all," Remi started. "Neither of you get me. I'm a person, not something you can 'get'. You two really are cavemen, you know," she accused. Remi wrapped her arms around Jag's neck and kissed her way into his mouth. She broke their kiss and leaned over his body to give Texas the same attention. Jag grabbed handfuls of Remi's ass and she squealed and wiggled against his palms.

"So, no one is being kicked to the curb?" Jag asked. His heart felt like it was racing and he worried that Remi would be able to feel just how nervous he was.

"No," she said. "No kicking and no curb," Remi teased.

"Then what the fuck is happening here?" Jag asked. He shot Tex an accusatory look.

Tex held up his hands and smiled. "Hey, don't look at me like that, man. We talked, just like you wanted and well, things happened." Texas smiled at Remi and she giggled. "Um, things happened a few times, so far tonight."

"Way to rub it in, man," Jag grumbled.

"This was all your idea," Texas said. "And, now your mad?" No, he wasn't mad. Hell, Jag was the opposite of angry. If he was being completely honest, he was relieved. When he left yesterday, he worried that Remi would never give either of them the time of day. He was in too deep with her not to have another chance. But, he also knew that the thing between him and Remi would only work if Texas was in the mix. Jag saw the way she looked at him, their night together. He also saw the uncertainty in Tex's eyes every time he watched her with Jag. It was Tex's way. He never thought he was good enough for anyone and Jag knew that it stemmed from Texas' father choosing the bottle over him. That shit would be enough to fuck up any kid. But, Tex wasn't that same boy who was shipped off to a foster home because his dad couldn't get his shit together and take care of his only kid.

"I'm not mad," he sighed. "Just surprised is all."

"Are you jealous?" Remi asked. Jag thought back over the past forty-eight hours, to the time he spent alone with Remi, and he had to admit, he wasn't jealous at all. He liked the idea of him and Tex each getting to spend one on one time with Remi. It would be a good idea for them to get to know her as well as they knew each other. The only way they'd do that would be to find some personal connection with her.

"No," Jag whispered. "You and I had a night alone together. It's only fair that you and Texas connect too."

"Really?" Texas asked.

"Really," Jag said. "Honestly, it can only make the three of us stronger if we have a one on one connection with Remi." Jag pulled Remi's body between the two of them, just the place they usually liked their women. "You sure you want this?" he asked. When she left him without a word he was sure he'd never hear from her again.

"I think I'd like to try, well—whatever this is that's happening between us. You guys in?" She looked up at the two of them and Jag knew for certain that neither of them would tell her no.

"Yes," Texas breathed.

"Me too," Jag sighed. Remi squealed and clapped like a child who had just won a prize.

"How about we start this little, whatever this is, tonight. I need a shower first," Jag said.

"Perfect man, I need to finish what I started with our girl and then we'll join you in the shower." Jag nodded and stripped. "That works, but I'm using your shower." He helped himself, walking back to Tex's bathroom. Smiling to himself when he heard the growl that ripped through Tex's chest, followed by the eruption of giggles from Remi. It had been a damn long day and Jag was looking forward to something finally going right in his life. Remi Nez cuddled between he and Tex felt pretty damn right.

****

The three of them spent the night tangled up together and Jag had to admit that he liked what was happening between the three of them. He knew that Remi didn't want to be pushed into giving their relationship a name, but that was exactly what it was becoming—a relationship.

Jag slept in later than usual and when he finally rolled out of bed, the smell of coffee and bacon led him down to the kitchen. He found Remi in just his t-shirt and Texas was wearing a shit-eating grin that was infectious.

"You two look disgustingly happy," Jag accused. He grabbed the coffee pot and poured himself a mug of coffee.

"Fair warning, Baby," Texas said, pulling Remi against his body. "Jag is a complete douche until at least his third cup of coffee." Remi giggled and crossed the kitchen to wrap her arms around Jag and kissed his cheek.

"Morning," she whispered, nuzzling his neck. He made a humming noise and she laughed. "I get it, Jag. I'm not much of a morning person, either.

"Great," Texas grumbled. "I'm the only one then."

"Yeah—well, hate to break it to you but not everyone can be stupidly happy about waking up every day. I mean, who rolls out of bed smiling?" Jag looked at his friend like he was a lunatic and Texas laughed.

"There isn't anything wrong with waking up happy, man. I had plenty of mornings that I woke up in prison and had nothing to be happy about. I'm free, I live with my best friend, I have a club I love being a part of and a sexy as fuck woman in my bed now—I'm good." Texas framed Remi's body between the two of them and Jag reveled in the fact that she seemed to fit so perfectly between them.

"You told her about doing time?" Jag mock whispered. Texas didn't share his back story with many people. Hell, he usually didn't let anyone get close enough to him to find out about his past.

"Yeah," Texas admitted. "We both laid it all out last night—both of our ugly pasts." Jag suddenly felt that he had a lot of catching up to do. He could tell that Remi had been through something dark and awful, but he didn't want to push her for details. He wanted her to come to him and willingly tell him her story, but in just one day Remi had opened up to Texas and they had shared personal shit he'd missed out on.

"Well," he said, clearing his throat. "That's great," he lied. "I'm going to shower and get ready for work. Excuse me." Jag stood and put his half-full cup of coffee into the sink and started from the kitchen. He'd get his coffee fix on the way into the hanger. He had some mechanical shit that needed to be addressed and then he needed to file his flight plans for next week's clients.

"Jag," Remi called after him. "What about breakfast?"

"Let him go, Honey. He's sulking. When he gets this way it's best to leave him alone," Texas said. "It's just his way."

Jag was sick of people telling him how he should act or what he should do. It was something he had to endure in the military, but now, that stuff just pissed him off. "I don't need you to explain me to Remi," he said, turning to face them both again. He took two menacing steps towards them and Remi snuggled into Texas' body as if she was afraid of Jag. Tex tugged her closer and smiled as if he liked the way she was turning to him for comfort.

"I wasn't trying to explain anything, man," Texas said. "You're just in a mood this morning."

"I'm not in a fucking mood. Hell, I think that I've been pretty easy going, all things considered."

"What the hell does that mean?" Remi questioned. It was one of the things that turned him on most about her. She was fierce and never backed down from anyone or anything.

"It means that we spent the night together after Tex took off, and you never told me one damn thing about yourself. Hell, when morning came, you couldn't seem to get out of my bed fast enough, Remi. So, yeah, maybe I sound like I'm accusing you of something. I don't know what's up anymore because no one is letting me in on any of your little secrets. Do you know how long it took Tex to tell me about being in prison? And, judging by the way you two are cozier than two peas in a fucking pod, I'm betting you told him whatever your dark secret is that haunts you." He paused and looked Remi over, knowing he hit his mark from the sadness he saw in her hazel eyes. That was the last thing Jag wanted—to cause her any sadness, but here he was, doing just that.

"Yeah," Texas admitted. "We both laid it all out last night—both of our ugly pasts." Jag suddenly felt that he had a lot of catching up to do. He could tell that Remi had been through something dark and awful, but he didn't want to push her for details. He wanted her to come to him and willingly tell him her story, but in just one day Remi had opened up to Texas and they had shared personal shit he'd missed out on.

"Well," he said, clearing his throat. "That's great," he lied. "I'm going to shower and get ready for work. Excuse me." Jag stood and put his half-full cup of coffee into the sink and started from the kitchen. He'd get his coffee fix on the way into the hanger. He had some mechanical shit that needed to be addressed and then he needed to file his flight plans for next week's clients.

"Jag," Remi called after him. "What about breakfast?"

"Let him go, Honey. He's sulking. When he gets this way it's best to leave him alone," Texas said. "It's just his way."

Jag was sick of people telling him how he should act or what he should do. It was something he had to endure in the military, but now, that stuff just pissed him off. "I don't need you to explain me to Remi," he said, turning to face them both again. He took two menacing steps towards them and Remi snuggled into Texas' body as if she was afraid of Jag. Tex tugged her closer and smiled as if he liked the way she was turning to him for comfort.

"I wasn't trying to explain anything, man," Texas said. "You're just in a mood this morning."

"I'm not in a fucking mood. Hell, I think that I've been pretty easy going, all things considered."

"What the hell does that mean?" Remi questioned. It was one of the things that turned him on most about her. She was fierce and never backed down from anyone or anything.

"It means that we spent the night together after Tex took off, and you never told me one damn thing about yourself. Hell, when morning came, you couldn't seem to get out of my bed fast enough, Remi. So, yeah, maybe I sound like I'm accusing you of something. I don't know what's up anymore because no one is letting me in on any of your little secrets. Do you know how long it took Tex to tell me about being in prison? And, judging by the way you two are cozier than two peas in a fucking pod, I'm betting you told him whatever your dark secret is that haunts you." He paused and looked Remi over, knowing he hit his mark from the sadness he saw in her hazel eyes. That was the last thing Jag wanted—to cause her any sadness, but here he was, doing just that.

"Fuck," Texas swore. "You have no right to talk to her like that, man."

"I have every right because I'm a part of this—whatever it is. Isn't that what we all agreed on last night? That we were all going to try to make this thing work between us?" Remi crossed the kitchen to stand in front of him. Jag was surprised Tex let her do it.

"You are," she whispered. "We are. I was putting up walls, not letting Texas in and he convinced me that it's alright not to be perfect. God, Jag, I'm far from perfect," she sobbed.

"We all are," Jag offered. He pulled her against his body and kissed the top of her head. "I just want to be a part of this—remember? Whatever this is."

Remi sighed and wrapped her arms around his waist. "You are a part of this, Jag," she promised. Remi cupped his cock and gasped when she found him already hard. "You're a huge part of this," she teased. Jag could see her putting her defenses back up and that hurt his damn feelings. How could she completely share herself with Tex and shut him out? Remi was hiding behind sex and that was the last thing he wanted. Sure, he was always up for a good fuck but if they didn't get down to what had her hiding from him, they'd never get past just falling into bed together. They'd never be more than what they were right now.

"Don't," Jag ordered.

"Don't what?" Remi whispered.

"Don't hide from him, Honey," Texas said. She let Texas pin her body between his and Jag's. "You can tell him what you've told me, Baby. Jag won't judge you; I promise."

"He won't want me if he finds out," she whispered.

"Try me," Jag said. He knew that letting Remi go would be damn near impossible for him at this point, he just wished she knew that.

"Just give him a chance, Remi," Tex said. "Let him prove to you that he wants in." Jag did too. He wanted to be a part of the two of them more than anything. "It's alright, Honey," Jag lied. "You can tell me when you're ready to." Jag kissed her forehead and turned to leave the kitchen.

"Where are you going?" Texas asked.

"I have to get to the hanger," he said. "Busy day," he lied. Jag didn't miss the flash of disappointment in Remi's hazel eyes. Maybe if he stayed, she'd tell him what she had shared with Tex, but he didn't want to stand around and hope that would happen. No, this time, he'd be the one to walk out—just as Texas and Remi had done to him. It was time for Jag to start to figure out his shit and putting a little distance between the three of them might be the best way to do that. At least, that was what he'd tell himself.

# TEXAS

"Fuck," Texas growled. He watched Jag run out of there like his ass was on fire and when Remi heard his bike leave the garage, she looked about ready to break down and cry. "He just needs some time, Remi. He'll be back," Texas offered. He didn't know if what he was saying was true or not, but that was all he had to give her—promises that might never be.

"I get it, this is happening so fast, he just needs a minute. I have to head back to my house to shower and change for work," Remi said. Tex hated that she was running too, but he had her for longer than he thought he would.

"You can use my shower," he offered.

"No, it's fine. I need a change of clothes and I should check in on Nena." Texas gave her the distance she seemed to be needing. She was fidgeting with the dishes and he knew she was just avoiding making eye contact with him.

"When can I see you again?" he asked. He worried that if he let her walk out of his house, she'd keep on going and he'd never see her again. Sure, he knew where she worked now at least, but he wasn't a stalker.

Remi stopped washing the dishes long enough to smile up at him. "I'm not really sure," she said. Tex felt as if his damn heart was going to stop. He was sure that this was the part where she told him that his time with her was up. What Remi didn't understand was that he'd fight like hell to have just one more night with her—and to hell with whatever shit Jag had going on.

"What the fuck, Remi? What the hell do you mean by that?" he asked.

She set the last dish in the drainer to dry and turned towards him, giving him her full attention. "Don't get yourself all worked up, Texas. I just meant that I'm going home for a few days with Oryana. Our aunt is sick and she has to have a few tests run. Her daughters will be with her, but someone needs to stay with Anali. Nena and I decided that a trip home would do us both some good."

"When do you leave?" he asked. Texas had a feeling he wasn't going to like her answer.

"Tonight," she admitted. "After work."

"Shit, Remi," he grumbled, swiping his hand down his face. How was he going to tell Jag that Remi up and left? Hell, how was he going to get his best friend to agree to give her a chance if she wasn't around to do just that? "When the hell were you going to tell us?"

"Hmm," she hummed. "Well, let me think." Remi tapped her finger against her chin as if she was deep in thought and then stared him down as if daring him to question her. "How about never. I don't owe either of you an explanation of my whereabouts. We've slept together twice," she said. "That hardly qualifies you or Jag to know where I am and what I'm doing. Hell, Jag isn't even speaking to me right now. How am I supposed to tell him about my trip home if he can't seem to be in the same room with me?"

Texas nodded, "I get that," he said. "You just took me by surprise. When will you be home?"

"Not sure, really," Remi said. She took the two steps to close the distance between them and wrapped her arms around his neck. "How about I call you when I'm back in town and we can hook-up?"

Texas wanted to protest the fact that she was only offering him a hook-up. He wanted more with her. Tex thought they had broken down a few of her barriers last night, but he was obviously wrong. He worried that protesting her word choice or admitting that he wanted more than just a hook-up with her would push Remi to balk at the idea. She seemed determined to keep him and Jag in the casual zone of whatever was happening between them. It sucked, but Tex would take her any way he could get her. Sooner or later, he hoped to tear down her walls and get her to admit that they were becoming more than just a one-night stand. If he had his way, he'd have Remi every fucking night.

"Fine," he agreed, not trying to give away his disappointment. "In the meantime, I'll try to figure out what the hell is up with Jag and try to talk him off whatever ledge he's on now."

"Thanks, Tex," Remi said. "I have to get going if I don't want to be late for work. We good here?" she asked. Texas wanted to tell her he wasn't good with any part of what she had just said, but there wasn't any way he'd send her off on a bad note. He at least wanted some fighting chance that Remi would call him when she got back into town.

"Yep," he lied and watched her disappear down the hall to his bedroom. He pulled his cell phone out of his jeans and called Jag. He wasn't sure Jag would even pick up and when he finally did, Tex knew that his friend was still pissed about their morning.

"What," Jag growled into the other end of the cell.

"Geeze man," Texas grumbled. "You really need to work on your phone manners."

"What do you want Tex? I'm really not in the mood for whatever this is," Jag warned.

"We need to talk, face to face," Texas said.

"Great," Jag shot back. "I'll be home tonight and we can talk then. Or, you can find me at Reckoning later. Either works for me, man."

Texas knew that time wasn't their friend. He worried that if he let Remi go home to New Mexico, things between the three of them might take a turn. Hell, Jag and Remi were already on shaky ground and Texas wanted to fix it—all of it. He didn't just want to, he needed to. In just two short days, Remi had come to mean something to him and he wasn't sure he'd be able to let her go. Not now.

"Tonight will be too late, Jag," Texas said. "Give me just ten minutes. I'll even come to you." Jag's hanger was at the local airport and about twenty miles out of his way, but what choice did he have? Texas knew that getting Jag to agree to anything when he was in a mood like this, would be nearly impossible. Offering to go to him might be the only way to get him to listen to reason.

He could hear Jag's heavy breathing on the other end of the line and he knew his friend was either really pissed or runny a marathon. Texas had a feeling it was his first guess. "Fine," Jag spat into the phone. "Ten minutes," he said and ended the call.

****

Texas walked Remi to her car and when she kissed his cheek and told him she'd see him soon; he didn't believe her for a second. He could see it in her eyes, she had already written him off and was putting all her walls back up. Telling him about losing her daughter and being raised by her grandmother and aunt—that was all for nothing. She had let him in only to shut him completely out again and fuck, it hurt.

He made it over to the airport in record time, deciding to ditch his truck and take his bike. He always kept a spare suit at the office, in case of an emergency and talking to Jag qualified as a damn emergency. He needed to get Jag's head screwed on right before he went and fucked up this whole thing with Remi. Jag stuck his head out from the hanger as if he wondered who was showing up, but Tex knew the score. Jag had probably been waiting for him since his phone call. It was who his best friend was—a worrier, an overthinker and sometimes, too damn caring for his own good. It wasn't like him to treat Remi the way he had that morning. Jag wouldn't have pushed her away like he had unless something was up. Texas just hoped Jag was in a sharing mood because he didn't have time to play twenty questions since he was on a tight schedule.

"Hey man," Tex shouted. "You here?" He already knew the answer, but he'd play Jag's game.

"Yeah," Jag grumbled from the back of the hanger. "I'm back here." Texas walked back to meet him and instantly knew that Jag hadn't cooled down from his earlier tantrum. He was standing next to a big metal desk he kept in the corner, in his make-shift office. Jag didn't bother with niceties, like actually looking up from the paperwork he was pretending to work on.

"What's up?" Texas casually asked.

"I don't know. You were the one who called me and insisted we had to talk. So, what's up, Texas?" Jag asked.

Tex chuckled and Jag shot him a look that told him he wasn't amused by the whole scene. "Okay," Texas said, holding up his hands in defense. "I just wanted to find out what the hell happened this morning. You treated Remi like crap and then ran out of the house like your ass was on fire."

"Yeah well, I'm done with being on the outside of whatever it is you two have going on." Jag set his paperwork down on his desk, giving Tex his full attention and he wished his friend would go back to pretending to be distracted by his flight plans. "What the hell was that this morning?" Jag asked.

Texas knew that Remi not sharing with him had hurt Jag's feelings. But he didn't even give her a chance to come clean. "You beat out of there so fast; you didn't give Remi or me a chance to explain."

"Explain what, exactly?" Jag slumped down into his chair and watched Texas as if expecting an answer to his question.

"I won't share Remi's story. That is for her to tell you and if you had given her a chance, she might have. But, I can tell you that we have a lot in common. Her parents aren't in the picture and well, you were right. Our girl has been through hell and back."

"Hell and back? Like what are we talking about here?" Jag questioned.

"Not my story to tell, man. I'm just worried she won't let you in now," Texas admitted. "I'm worried she won't let either of us in."

"Why the fuck not?" Jag asked.

"She's put her walls up and she's running, man," Tex growled.

"Running where?" Jag asked.

"She said she's going home, with Nena. Something about her aunt being sick and needing some tests. She and Nena are going back to be with her grandmother." Jag pushed the papers around on his desk and then stood and cursed.

"You sure?" Jag asked. "How do you know she's running and not just going home for a visit as she said?"

"A feeling, I guess. Fuck, I don't know," Texas admitted. "I just know that she was acting differently after you left. I asked her when we'd see her again and she said she wasn't sure."

"All that means is her schedule is up in the air," Jag defended. "Maybe you're just reading too much into it."

"No," Texas breathed. "You trust me, Jag?" he asked.

It was nice that Jag didn't seem to miss a beat before he answered. "Yes," Jag agreed. "With my life."

"Great," Texas said. "Then how about you give me a little faith here and help me come up with a fucking plan to keep our girl from running off and shutting us out of her life?"

"She's not our girl," Jag grumbled.

"You keep telling yourself that, man. Remi's been our woman since the night she walked into Reckoning, to tell Lyra that she was in danger. You need to get your head out of your ass and give her a chance, man. Give the three of us a fighting chance here, Jag. I'm falling for her and if I had to bet on it—I'd say that you are too." Texas stared him down as if challenging him to deny it. Jag didn't. He didn't need to because Tex could see it in his eyes every time Jag looked at Remi. He was all in where she was concerned.

"So, how about it, man? Are we going to New Mexico to convince our woman to give us both a chance? I figure you can do some groveling, to get back into Remi's good graces, and I'll sit back and enjoy the show. I'm pretty sure she'll give you some shit before she agrees to forgive you. At least, that's what I'm hoping for."

"Yeah, yeah," Jag grumbled. "When does she leave?"

"Tonight, after work," Texas said.

"Fine, we leave in the morning. I have a few things to do today and I'm having the mechanic look at the landing gear. As soon as I get the all-clear, we can take off." Texas knew that his fist-bumping the air was too much, but he didn't give a fuck. He was excited about their little trip and if he was right, they'd come back home with their woman just where she belonged—between the two of them.

## REMI

Remi hated that Oryana wouldn't let her drive. Her sister had to be exhausted and it was her turn, but Nena refused to give up the driver's seat. "I took a three-hour nap—I'm good, Nena," Remi pleaded.

"You know I get car sick," Remi," Nena countered.

"You haven't gotten sick in a car since we were eight, Nena." Her sister flashed her evil grin and Remi knew she was fighting a losing battle. When Nena wanted something, she really knew how to throw down and dig her heels in. They were a lot alike in that way.

"Fine," Remi spat. "Suit yourself, but don't come crying to me when you're tired and need a break. You can just drive the whole way there."

"Deal," Nena quickly agreed and Remi wondered if that wasn't her sister's plan all along. Oryana giggled, telling her that she had correctly guessed what her twin was up to. "Don't look like such a sore loser, Remi," Nena said. Remi didn't even try to hide her scowl, causing her sister to laugh harder.

"You have always been a cheater, even when it comes to tricking me into giving you your way," Remi accused. She crossed her arms over her chest, even making a small "humphing" noise, only making Nena giggle louder.

"And you've always been a sore loser," Nena accused. "Let's listen to some music." Nena didn't wait for Remi to agree; turning on the radio. They had about ten more hours to drive and Remi worried that this was going to feel like the longest trip of her life.

"Tell me again why we didn't fly?" Remi mumbled more to herself than Nena.

Um, well, because we have no money saved and this was a spur of the moment trip. Still, I feel you, Sis. It's no picnic being trapped in the car with you for almost seventeen straight hours. You're quite the sour puss," Nena accused. She wanted to act put out by her sister's assessment, but Nena was right. She was acting like a sour puss and that had everything to do with Jag walking away from her that morning, not even giving her a chance to explain what had happened between her and Tex. If he had, she would have told him everything—about her parents and about Aria. But, he so effortlessly shoved her aside and only seemed to care about his own feelings, she was now rethinking everything that had happened between the three of them. Remi needed this trip home, not just to see her family, but to hopefully blow off some steam and figure out her next move with Jag and Texas.

"Want to talk about it?" Nena asked. "Afterall, we do have like ten hours to kill."

"More like eleven or twelve, with your pit stops," Remi accused.

"Hey, I have a small bladder," Nena defended.

"And a love for all things fast food and caffeine," Remi said. "Don't pretend otherwise, Nena. Remember who you're talking to here. I know you better than anyone," Remi reminded.

"That's true," Nena agreed. "And right back at you, Sis. So, how about you share what or I'm guessing who, in this case, has you in such a pissed-off mood." Remi knew that denying that Jag and Tex were behind her current mood would be a mistake. Once her sister picked up the scent, she was like a dog with a bone.

"Fine," she sighed. "I'm not really sure what's going on with them. One minute, we are hot and heavy and the next, one of them ends up pissed off about something and storms off. I'm getting whiplash at their mood swings. I think I need to maybe take a step back. Hell, maybe I should just move on."

"You like them?" Nena asked. Her sister always had a way of cutting right to the chase.

"I don't know—yeah, I think I do, but I'm also afraid to like them too much. What happens if I fall for them and they decide I'm not worth it?" Remi questioned. That was always her biggest fear—people finding out that she was a total fraud. She had let her own daughter down and ended up losing her. She wanted to keep that part of her life buried deep down but telling Texas about Aria felt right. He didn't judge her; even told her it wasn't her fault. Remi knew the truth though—it was. She should have been paying attention instead of trying to help everyone else around her.

"You're worth it, Remi. I think that maybe it's time to stop beating yourself up and let someone in. Well, in this case, two someones." Nena bobbed her eyebrows at Remi, making her laugh.

"I'll think about it if you think about letting me drive some of this trip," Remi taunted. She knew her sister's stubborn streak would give out and she'd either let her drive or find a cheap motel for them to stay in.

"Yeah, we'll see," Nena said.

****

They drove through most of the night and when Oryana couldn't seem to keep her eyes open, she found a motel with a vacant room and they checked in to catch a few hours' sleep.

Sharing a bed with Nena wasn't ever fun, but Remi made the best of it. They only had one available room, with a double bed. Honestly, she was so tired, she would have slept in the car, but the bed was comfy. She'd just find a way to get around Nena's snoring.

"Hey Sis," Nena whispered. Remi looked around and it was completely dark. Just a dimly lit overhead light showed her sister's face.

"Where are we?" Remi asked. She hated staying in strange locations. Waking up and not knowing where she was always made her uneasy. It was one of the reasons she didn't like to stay over at a guy's place. Remi always got dressed and made some excuse as to why she had to leave so quickly. That was until she met Jag and Tex. She had spent the entire night with them and waking up in the morning, with the two hunky bikers, set her nerves on edge. She had woken up and wanted to run out of their house so fast, it would have made their heads spin. It's what she did to poor Jag a few days prior and the look of hurt on his face nearly broke her damn heart.

"I'm not sure," Nena admitted. She looked around as if trying to get her bearings and Remi did the same. "I think we're in some sort of parking lot," Nena said, pointing to the few cars that were scattered around the lot.

Remi looked around and noticed the white van before they could hear the woman's muffled shouts coming from it. Nena took a step towards the van and Remi put her hand on her sister's shoulder, as if trying to stop her.

"Nena," she whispered. "This is a vision. I think we just found someone. Get as much information as possible."

Nena smiled and nodded, "It's not my first rodeo, Sis. Let's do this." Nena took her hand and they walked over to the van, sliding open the side door. Usually, when they had a vision, they were merely spectators, looking on. It was like they were watching a movie from the inside, but they weren't a part of the cast. They found a woman with long, dark hair naked in the back of the van. She was lying on her side and her ankles and wrists were bound with rope. Her hair looked matted with blood and she had dried blood crusted to one side of her face. It was all they could see since her back was towards them.

"Who are you?" Nena asked. "We want to help you." The woman turned to look back at them, her mouth had been covered with silver duct tape, but Remi knew those eyes. They belonged to her cousin. Why the fuck would someone do this to her cousin?

"Aylen?" she questioned.

"Oh my God, Ay. Tell us what happened," Nena insisted. She

rolled Aylen over, to face them, pulling the duct tape free from her mouth. Her sob was nearly a howl and it damn near broke Remi's heart.

"Oh Ay," Remi cried, wrapping her jacket around her little cousin's naked body. Nena looked for something to help loosen Aylen's bindings and found a knife in the passenger seat. Remi took it from her and sliced through the rope, freeing her cousin.

"Tell us," Remi demanded. "How does this happen to you?"

"It already has," Aylen sobbed. "You can't stop this."

"Who did this?" Nena asked.

"I'm—I'm not sure," she stuttered. "A man stopped me on my way out of work. He pulled up to the curb when I was going to the parking garage. He pretended to be lost and asked me for directions. I told him I wasn't sure about the area he was going to and he got angry. He pulled a knife from somewhere under his seat and told me to get into the back of the van."

"Oh God," Remi cried. "Where are you now? Can you describe him?"

"Give her a minute," Nena said.

"Thanks," Aylen said. "I knew you guys would find me in my dreams. I knew if I could find a way to connect with you both, you'd be able to find me." Aylen paused and she frantically looked around, as if expecting to see her assailant. "He got out of his van and chased me down and God, he told me that he would slit my throat if I screamed. So, I didn't."

"It's alright, Ay. You're safe now. Can you tell us anything else?"

"He's bald and looked to be in his fifties. He knew my name. I think he works at the hospital too, and that's how he knew who I am." Aylen was the first one in their family to go to college and actually graduate. Hell, she more than just graduated—she was a doctor. An orthopedist, to be exact, and she was damn good at her job.

"Where do you think he has you?" Remi asked. She looked around the area, searching for a road sign or any landmarks that might give away where Aylen was being held. They looked to be in a heavily wooded area, at what seemed to be an old rest stop. The parking lot had just a few cars in it, besides the van that held her cousin.

"I'm not really sure," Aylen admitted. "It felt like he drove us around for hours, but I'm guessing it was more like thirty minutes or so. He parked the van here and put tape over my mouth, telling me that he had to cover his tracks, so no one would be able to follow us. He said he'd be back and I'm afraid that when he gets here, he'll move me—or worse. I overheard him talking on his cell, while we were driving, and he said something about a high bidder. I'm afraid he's going to sell me," Aylen admitted.

Remi knew all too well about the threat of human trafficking, especially of Native American women. She had worked with an agency in New Mexico, that helped women find their way in life after they were saved from that nightmare. The abduction of Native American women accounted for forty percent of human trafficking. In New Mexico, one-quarter of all abducted women were Native and it broke Remi's heart to hear each and every one of their stories. She couldn't let that happen to Aylen or anyone she loved.

"We won't let that happen," she promised her cousin.

"Remi," Nena warned. She knew better than to make promises she might not be able to keep, but she couldn't help herself—it was Aylen. Her cousin was like her younger sister. It was just her and Nena until their Aunt Joanna took them in and made them a part of her family. She had two daughters—Kaiah was the same age as her and Nena, but Aylen was just an infant. Remi fell immediately in love with her little cousin. She used to pretend that Ay was her little sister and that drove Kaiah crazy. It was probably the reason her cousin seemed to take great pleasure in pointing out that Joanna wasn't her and

Nena's mother. They knew that, but Kaiah seemed to need to remind them of that fact, every chance she got.

"Please guys, you can't let him sell me. Find me, please," Aylen begged.

"We will do everything we can, Ay," Nena promised. "We'll be home by morning if we wake up now." Remi worried that they were going to be the ones to break the news about Aylen's abduction to their aunt and grandmother. How were they going to do that? How did they break news like that to the people they loved most in the world?

"Wake up," Aylen said. She put on a brave smile as tears fell down her blood-stained cheeks. She nodded and turned her back to them, assuming the position they had found her in, legs and arms bound and duct tape back over her mouth. It broke Remi to leave her cousin that way, but their conversation with Aylen was based on an illusion. That was always the way, having to figure out what was real and what wasn't, during their visions. Remi knew that somewhere her cousin was lying in a van, hand, and feet bound, duct tape over her mouth, scared out of her mind. Remi was just thankful that Aylen had been able to fall asleep long enough to connect with them. If the situation was reversed, she wasn't sure she'd be able to do that.

"See you soon, cousin," she whispered and opened her eyes. It was time to finish their trip home and find her cousin. She and Nena had a promise to keep.

## JAG

Jag tossed and turned most of the night and by the time the sun came up, he wanted to wake Tex and tell him that he was ready to take off, literally. He had called the hanger, to make sure that everything was clear for their trip. He was given the thumbs up to fly and he had to admit, he was pretty damn anxious to get to New Mexico. He'd never admit it to Texas, but he was right. Tex would never let him live that fact down. They did need to have a come to Jesus meeting with Remi and lay down a few truths. The first being that they needed open communication between the three of them if this thing was going to have a chance to work. No more hiding or running. They were all guilty of both and it was time for them to be completely open and honest with each other. The next thing they needed to get straight was that she was theirs, whether she knew it or not. They were both falling for her and he'd do just about anything to hear her admit the same thing to him and Tex.

Texas threw their duffel bags onto the plane and smiled at him. "Good thing we travel light, man. Maybe you can fly us to New Mexico faster and we can claim our woman by nightfall." He bobbed his eyebrows at Jag, causing him to chuckle.

"Is she?" Jag asked. "You know—our woman. She's shut us down at every turn. I thought I had broken through her barriers the night we spent together, over Reckoning. The next morning, she couldn't seem to get dressed and run out of our room fast enough. Then, she shows up at our house and spends the night between the two of us, sharing her body, but not letting me in completely."

"I'm sorry about that, man. I still think I'm doing the right thing here. Remi's story is her's to tell, not mine. Please just trust that she's been through a lot of shit, man. She's been torn apart by life and she's just trying to find a way to hang on."

"How?" Jag asked.

"Well, I think she runs from relationships, for starters. She said she doesn't spend more than one night with a guy. She's given us two nights now, so there's that. Baby steps, man. That's what we all need to focus on now. We'll get there; but first, we need to find her," Tex said.

Jag nodded, "Let's get going then. I have a feeling that Remi's going to give us a fight and we're burning daylight."

****

The flight was short and by the time they landed and hunted down Remi's family's address, it was nearly dinner time. Texas rented a truck for them and drove out to her grandmother's house. It took calling in a few favors with his military connections, but Jag was able to get the information they needed. Remi's grandmother lived just outside of town if that's what he would call the little strip of buildings that ran about a half-mile down the road. Honestly, he'd never been in a place so desolate in his life, outside of the warn torn countries he had to live in while serving his time in the Air Force.

"She lives out in the middle of nowhere," Texas grumbled. It felt that way. They had been driving for about an hour now and Jag was tired and ready to have the conversation with Remi that was way overdue.

"Is that it, up there?" Jag asked pointing to the little single-story house.

"Man, I hope so," Tex said.

"You think Remi and Nena made it here yet?" Jag asked. He hated that they drove almost seventeen hours from NOLA. He would have gladly flown them out to see their grandmother and aunt.

"No idea, but I think she'll be able to tell us," Texas said, nodding to the older woman who stood on the front porch that ran the length of the small house. "I'm guessing that's her grandmother."

Jag jumped out of the rental as soon as Texas pulled up to the house. "Hello," he called to the older woman. We're looking for Remi and Nena."

"I know who you are," the woman said. "I saw you were coming for my granddaughter, Remi.

"You must be her Anali," Texas said, holding out his hand. He was putting on his country boy charm and when Remi's grandmother ignored Tex's extended hand, Jag belted out his laugh.

"I think I like her," Jag whispered.

"I'm worried about my girls," the old woman admitted. She looked like she had been crying. Her long gray hair framed her round face and Jag didn't miss the way she watched them both.

"They haven't shown up here yet?" Texas asked.

"They got here early this morning. The twins had a vision over-night and they're worried about their cousin, Aylen." Jag was having trouble keeping up with the older woman. Her thoughts seemed scattered and he was beginning to think she wasn't in her right mind. "Don't look at me like that, boy. I'm making complete sense," she said as if reading his thoughts.

Jag held his hands up in defense. "Okay, how about we slow down and start from the beginning. Remi and Nena got home this morning, right?"

"Yes," she breathed. He could tell that he was getting on her nerves, but if she was correct and Remi was in some sort of trouble, he wanted to be able to help.

"Then what happened?" Tex asked.

"The twins told me that they had a vision last night. I'm assuming Remi has told you about what our family can do?" Jag and Tex both nodded, not wanting to interrupt her. "They saw their cousin, Aylen, in a vision they shared and she had been abducted."

"Well, can't they just warn her and then change it from happening?" Texas questioned. "I mean, we're not experts on the whole seer thing, but that's what Remi did for Jag here, a couple of nights ago. She saw his death and well—stopped it." Jag bit back his groan at the way Texas almost shared too much with Remi's grandmother. She saved his life by agreeing to spend the night between him and Tex. Telling her grandmother that wasn't something he wanted to do though.

The woman smiled at Texas. "Yes, I'm aware," she admitted and Jag had a sneaky feeling she knew a whole lot more than what they were telling her. "Nena and Remi believe the abduction has already occurred," she said.

"Have you tried to contact Aylen?" Jag asked. She smirked at him and nodded.

"Yeah," she said. "No one has seen or heard from her in almost a day now. Her sister, Kaiah is beside herself but she's staying with her mother. My daughter, Joanna, is in Texas having some tests run over the next few days. Both Aylen and Kaiah were supposed to go with her but Aylen never showed up. Joanna couldn't cancel her testing and we agreed that she should go. We're not telling her about what Nena and Remi saw, not until we have confirmation. There is no sense in worrying her without cause."

"So, where are Nena and Remi now?" Texas asked.

"They went to town this afternoon, to report Aylen as missing at the local police department. They should have been back by now," the woman said.

"And, that's why you're worried about them," Jag said.

"Yes. And, we just wasted all this time discussing details when you could have headed back to town to track down my girls," Remi's grandmother accused. Yeah, Jag liked her. She seemed like a tough woman who didn't take crap from anyone.
"So, we need to go back into town, as in twenty miles that way?" Tex pointed in the direction they had just come from and groaned.

"Yes," she agreed. "And, don't come back without the twins. I'm guessing that if they aren't still at the station, filing a missing person's report; they'll be at the only bar. The girls haven't been home for a few months and they'll want to catch up with their friends. If I know Remi, she'll be questioning everyone within a ten-mile radius about Aylen's disappearance."

Texas looked like he wanted to give her an argument but was smart enough to know better. He turned and started back to the rental.

"Let's go, man," Texas said. "The sooner we find Nena and Remi, the sooner we can figure this mess out."

****

They drove the twenty miles back to town and Jag had to admit, he was anxious to find Remi. If her cousin was in danger, he knew she would do just about anything to help her. It was one of the things he loved most about her—her heart and her willingness to help people. From what her grandmother told them, Aylen would need not only Remi and Nena's help but his and Tex's too. They would do whatever it took to help find Remi's missing cousin.

Texas stopped at the police station and they were told that the twins had been there, to file the missing person's report, earlier in the day. But, they had left and the lone officer on duty told them to head over to The Thirsty Eye, which was the town's only bar. The officer told them that he had it on good authority that the twins were over there, trying to track down Aylen. They thanked the guy and high tailed it over to the bar.

Tex parked in the back of the bar's parking lot and they went in to find Remi. "You think she's still here?" Tex asked. Honestly, Jag was so tired, he was ready to find their girl and head over to the hotel. He and Tex had found a vacancy at the only hotel in the area. Judging from the less than warm reception from Remi's grandmother, it was probably for the best.

"I don't know man," Jag grumbled. "I'm about ready to call it a fucking night though."

"I'm tired too, but Remi might need us," Texas said. He stopped short when they both seemed to spot their girl at the same time. She was in the back of the bar, on the dance floor, with her arms wrapped around a big, tattooed biker and Texas looked about ready to walk back to her and tear the unsuspecting guy apart.

"What the fuck," Tex growled.

"I'm leaving," Jag shouted over the music. "Fuck this."

"No," Texas said. "Let's hear her out first, man." Nena slipped from her bar stool and walked across the bar to them. She smiled up at Jag as if she was happy to see them, but her eyes told another story.

"What are you guys doing here?" she asked.

"We wanted to surprise Remi, but I think she's one-upped us on that front," Jag said. Nena looked across the bar to where her sister was making out with the very handsy guy and back to Jag. "I'm sorry you guys have to see her like this," she shouted. "It's been a rough day and she's just blowing off some steam."

"Is that what we're calling that?" Texas said, nodding over to Remi's display of PDA. The guy reached down and grabbed her ass, hauling her up his body to kiss her. Texas growled and shot across the barroom and Jag knew that there was going to be trouble, whether he was ready for it or not.

"Take your fucking hands off our woman," Texas yelled. The big guy, who currently had his hand's full of Remi's curvy ass, looked at Tex and smiled.

"Remi's mine tonight; beat it." He made a shooing motion with his left hand and Tex looked about ready to remove the guy's whole arm. Remi looked over her shoulder at the two of them and frowned; not quite the reaction either of them were hoping for.

"Listen Texas, maybe this is what Remi wants. Let's just go; this was all a huge mistake," Jag admitted. It was, too. Flying to New Mexico to fix something that was never meant to be was a big fucking mistake.

"No," Texas growled. "I want to hear it from her—Remi?" God, he hated how torn up Tex sounded about all of this. Jag knew—he realized what they both were to her. Remi used them to feel good for a couple of nights, but that was all. She wasn't really giving them a chance.

"We knew the score," Jag said. "She spent the night with us to save my life. We were nothing else to her. Am I right, Sweetheart?" His smile felt mean and he knew that he was being a complete ass, but he didn't give a fuck. It hurt to see the woman he wanted tangled up with some other man. It felt like a fucking knife to his gut hearing how torn up Texas was about finding Remi with the tattooed hulk. They were both hurting but he wasn't about to stand in the middle of that bar and fucking beg her to be theirs.

Remi turned to face them and the Neanderthal she was with had the nerve to band his arms around her middle and pull her back against his body. Texas let his frustrated growl rip from his chest, just as the music paused, and the entire bar seemed to take notice of their little scene.

"Stay cool, man," Jag loudly whispered. "We have eyes on us."

Remi seemed to notice their new audience and shyly ducked her head. "Can we please take this outside?" she asked. "These people are my friends."

"And what are we?" Texas growled. "Just two guys you fucked?"

"Tex," Jag warned. The caveman who was still holding her looked about ready to kill someone and from the way some of the guys in the bar started to crowd around them, he had friends who were willing to throw down for him.

"Please," Remi begged.

"Fine," Jag said. It looked like his options were to go outside and have a conversation he didn't want to have, or get the piss beat out of both him and Tex in the little dive bar. "But your new boyfriend stays here," Jag countered.

Remi looked up at the hulk and smiled and nodded. "I'll be fine, Butch," she offered. "They are friends from New Orleans." God, it stung to hear her call them "friends". They were so much more than just her fucking friends, but he'd explain that to her once they were away from every testosterone-fueled man in town. They swarmed around him and Tex and Jag knew that they were outnumbered and would end up with more than just a beating to deal with. Texas looked at Remi like a love-sick puppy and Jag wanted to tell his friend she wasn't worth it. He wanted to tell Tex that Remi wasn't worth the heart-ache or trouble she was causing them at every turn. That would be a lie though because she was. God help him, she was.

## REMI

Remi had spent the day filing a missing person's report for Aylen and begging anyone and everyone to believe her and Nena. They had proven their abilities over and over again but each time they had a new vision, it was almost like they had to start all over. Today was no different and she was mentally and physically exhausted. It didn't help that she had slept with the officer on duty a few years back. Hell, it probably cut down on her credibility with him, but finding her cousin was too important to back down just because she had a night of casual sex with the guy.

Nena finally stepped up and got him to believe them, but it still sucked. By the time they ended up at their favorite spot in town, all their friends were there waiting for them.

She and Nena had a plan to divide and conquer, asking each person if they had seen or heard from Aylen; but no one had. Kaiah had called home earlier and was beside herself with worry but they all agreed to keep Aunt Joanna in the dark about her daughter's disappearance until after her testing was done. There was no sense in worrying her before they had news.

Anali was beside herself with grief and worry. As soon as they showed up, they told their grandmother all the sorted details. Watching her grandmother become so distraught at not seeing Aylen's fate was awful. It was a feeling she knew herself, all too well. When she lost Aria, she had felt that way. Anali questioned why she herself had missed seeing something having to do with her own granddaughter. Remi hated the guilt she heard in her grandmother's pleas to find their cousin. Remi and Nena promised to bring Aylen home, but was that a promised they'd be able to keep? Remi was worried that it wasn't; especially after hitting so many brick walls today.

That's why when her old high school flame, Butch, asked her to dance tonight, she quickly agreed. All Remi wanted to do was lose herself in someone else. He offered her a means of escape and that was exactly what she needed. Mind-numbing sex with someone who didn't matter to her anymore. A means to forget seeing her younger cousin bound and gagged in that fucking van. A way to forget the fact that she and Nena were no closer to finding their cousin and keeping their promises to both Aylen and Anali. Remi never dreamed that both Tex and Jag would chase her half-way across the fucking country to find her in that little dive bar. She'd do just about anything to take away the hurt she saw in both of their eyes. It was the last thing she wanted to do—hurt them, but it was best that they learned who she had become now before they fell for her.

She followed Texas and Jag out to the parking lot, hoping to avoid having this conversation with an audience. The last thing she needed was the extra attention. She and Nena were so used to that unwanted attention, but the guys weren't. They needed to hear from her that she wasn't the person they thought she was. Jag and Texas were better off without her and the sooner they all realized that, the better off the three of them would be.

Remi spun around to face two very pissed off, sexy as fuck, bikers and her traitorous body seemed to hum to life.

"You want to tell us what the hell that was, Honey?" Texas barked.

"That was me blowing off some steam after a very bad day. That, Texas, was none of your business." Remi put her hands on her hips, trying for badass but falling short, according to the smirk on Jag's face. "Why are you smiling at me like that? Are you making fun of me, Jag?"

He held up his hands as if defending himself, "Naw," he drawled. "I'm just trying to figure out which of you two alpha dogs is gonna win this one. I have to admit that watching the two of you circle each other isn't boring."

"There is nothing funny about any of this," Remi insisted, stomping her foot for good measure. Yeah, she wasn't helping her case by acting like a complete child. Texas was now smiling at her just like Jag and she was having a hard time keeping a straight face. The three beers she had earlier weren't helping her either.

"Why are you guys even here?" Remi whispered. "I told you I'd be in touch when I got back to town," she said. Sure, it was a total lie, but the guys didn't know that.

"Right, Honey," Texas said. "I think you made it crystal clear about what your plans were. You had no intention of seeing us again because we force you out of your comfort zone."

Jag stared her down, "Is that what this is about? You're afraid that we'll tear down your walls, so you're shutting us out, Honey?" Jag asked. How could she admit that every time he started getting close to her, she'd push him away? She'd shut him down and put her mask back into place. It's who she had become since losing her daughter and she owed neither of them any apologies.

"No," she lied. "I'm just not the type of woman who wants a relationship. Things with me—well, they're complicated." They were too, but mostly because she chose to let them be that way between her and the two guys. It's how her life had to be because letting them in would mean that she'd have to give up some of her tightly held control and that couldn't happen.

"Is this because of Aria?" Texas asked. Remi gasped and took a step back from them both.

"How could you, Texas?" Remi spat. "I told you that in private."

"Who's Aria?" Jag asked. God, she didn't want to get into this here and now. She just wanted a night of fun and a way to forget that she'd messed up once again and someone she loved was now missing or possibly worse. She should have seen what happened to her cousin before it occurred, not after. Maybe, if she had been paying better attention and worrying less about ending up in bed with Texas and Jag, her cousin would be safe right now instead of bound and gagged in the back of some van.

Remi defiantly raised her chin. Facing Jag's simple question like it was a challenge. "Aria was my daughter."

"You have a kid?" Jag questioned. This was the part she always hated. Having to explain that she did have a daughter, but that she was careless and lost her baby girl. People always looked at her a little differently when she admitted that to them. It was always a cross between pity and despair that she saw in their eyes.

"I did," she admitted.

"Oh," Jag whispered, catching on. "I'm sorry."

"I am too, Remi," Texas offered. He reached for her, but she took another step back. "I didn't mean to blurt that out. Not like that, but we need to talk about this—about us."

Remi barked out her laugh, "There is no us," Tex," she almost shouted. "Can't you just accept that I was a one-night stand and move on?"

"Nope," he said, smiling triumphantly down at her. "We were a two-night stand," he corrected. Jag's scowl looked like he was finding the whole scene a lot less funny than Tex. He was always the serious one. She could sometimes feel him watching her, studying her and now was no exception. His blue eyes felt as though they were going to bore into her soul and Remi worried about what he'd find there.

"Please don't look at me like that, Jag," she whispered.

"Is this what you told Texas the other night? You two bonded over the fact that you lost your daughter, but you couldn't tell me? What the hell, Remi?" Jag looked about ready to punch someone and she had to admit, his anger was easier to deal with than his pity.

"Yes," she admitted. "That and the fact that we both grew up without a mom or dad in our lives."

"Fuck," Jag swore. "I didn't even have a chance, did I?"

"What does that mean?" Remi questioned.

"Well, I don't have some tragic story, so how can I compete?" Jag asked. Honestly, he was right. She knew close to nothing about him and that was on her. She hadn't taken the time to get to know Jag because if she had, she'd be giving him the power to rip her world apart. Every time he looked at her, she knew that he saw her—not some version of herself that she put out into the world for people to see. Jag and Tex were the only people in her life who could see straight through her bullshit.

"That's not fair, man," Texas said. She smiled up at him, thankful that he was trying to come to her rescue, but Jag was right.

"No, Texas—Jag's right. I never let you in and I'm sorry. I was afraid," Remi admitted.

"Of me?" Jag asked. "Of me not wanting you because of your past?"

"No," Remi answered. She wouldn't give him anything but her honesty now. She owed them both that and so much more. They had saved her and her sister's lives and Remi knew that lying to either of them now wasn't something she could do. "I was worried you'd want me—you know like you'd want to fix me. I'm broken, Jag and you're so—"

"So what?" he asked.

"So perfect," she whispered. "I worried that if I let you both into my world, you wouldn't want to let me go. I don't let my walls down for anyone—not even Nena. If I let them down for the two of you and something were to happen to either of you, it would kill me."

"You don't let people in because you're afraid that you'll lose them, the way you lost Aria?" Texas asked.

Remi didn't try to hide the small sob that escaped her chest at the mention of her little girl. "Yes," she cried. "I can't lose anyone else, but now—Aylen is missing and—" Remi's voice cracked and the guys didn't let her finish, pulling her between their bodies, cocooning her, making her feel completely safe between them.

"Stay with us," Jag whispered into her ear. "We're at the hotel down the road. We can talk or not, whatever you need, Honey. Stop shutting us out, Remi."

"What about Nena?" Remi asked.

"I'll take the car back and stay with Anali," her sister said, startling her.

"Nena," Remi yelped. "How long have you been standing there?"

"Long enough, Sis. You go with the guys and work things out. I'll take care of Anali. We can meet up in the morning, to start our search for Ay again." Nena didn't wait for her to answer. She kissed her cheek and walked to her car, not looking back.

"Well, she was my ride. So, I guess I'll take you up on your offer to stay with you," Remi said. She wasn't sure if spending the night with her two sexy bikers was a good idea or not, but she honestly didn't care. Remi needed them—both of them and for once, she was going to take what she wanted.

****

They got down to the town's only hotel and Remi cringed at seeing another one of her exes working the check-in desk. "Remi," Trevor said. He was always a smooth talker. It was one of the things she liked most about him and apparently, she wasn't alone in that. After they broke up, she found out that half the women in town had dated the silver-tongued Romeo. She couldn't blame him; she was a serial dater too and they both knew the score.

"Trev," she said, plastering on her best smile.

"Nena just stopped by here on her way back to your grandmother's place. She left this for you and said she thought you might need it." Trevor handed her the small suitcase she had brought along.

"Thanks," she said.

"Um, we have a room for the night," Jag interrupted.

"Just one room?" Trevor asked. Honestly, he sounded more like he was accusing them of something. "If that won't suit, I'm sure I can help find other accommodations for you, Remi." Texas looked about ready to pound poor Trevor into a pulp. She stepped between them and smiled up at Trevor again.

"Nope," she said. "No alternative accommodations needed Trev. Just the one room, please," she said, noting the way he looked her up and down as if weighing and measuring her. Jag took a protective step in front of her as if trying to block her from Trevor's assessments. "It's okay, Jag," she said. "I'm good."

Texas took her bag from her and held out his hand for hers. Remi took it and when Jag did the same, she took his hand too. "Key card?" Jag asked, holding out his free hand to Trevor.

"Yeah," Trevor stuttered. "Room two-twelve," he said. "If you need anything else, please let me know."

"Thanks, Trev," Texas said. "But, I think we're good for the night." They led Remi to the elevator and she didn't bother to look back at Trevor. She knew that judgment she'd find staring back at her and right now, she didn't give a fuck.

****

They found their room on the second floor and before Jag could even get the fucking door open, Tex had pushed her up against it, kissing his way into her mouth. God, she missed him. His raw need and the way he seemed to want to consume her set her girl parts on fire. Jag finally got the key card to work and opened the door. She and Tex practically fell into their small room and Jag kicked the door shut behind them. They threw the bags into the corner of the room and her guys surrounded her body, tangling her up between them. Remi wasn't sure where they ended and she began, giving her exactly what she needed from them both.

"Strip," Texas breathlessly ordered. Remi looked at him like he had lost his mind.

"Sorry, what?" she asked.

"I believe he said to strip, Honey," Jag said.

"Wait, I thought we'd discuss who's going to be in charge first," she asked. Texas pulled her back into his arms and she could tell that he wasn't going to take any of her shit tonight. He looked mad as hell still and she had a feeling that had everything to do with finding her wrapped up with her ex, on the dance floor.

"Yeah well, we also agreed to give things a chance to play out between the three of us and you went and let some asshole put his hands on you," Texas said. His accusations were like a bucket of cold water to her libido.

"Do you have any idea what that did to us, Remi? Finding you on the dance floor, letting some guy put his hands and fucking lips on your body?" Jag asked.

"I—I'm sorry," she stuttered. "I wasn't thinking." Remi covered her face with her hands, wanting to hide from them both. God, she was an ass. When she rolled into town and tried to find someone—anyone who would listen to her and Nena, she panicked when they were turned away by everyone she trusted. Everyone sent them packing, telling them that they would need to come up with more than just a vision or a hunch if they were going to be able to file a missing person's report. Having to call Anali, to tell her that they had failed, nearly broke her heart. Her grandmother reminded her and Nena that Aylen was counting on them as if either of them needed the reminder. Aylen was more than a cousin to her and Nena and they would do just about anything to bring her home safely.

Facing the fear of failure again made all of Remi's insecurities come flooding back and all she could think about doing was finding the first willing man and taking her frustrations out on him.

"Were you going to sleep with him?" Texas asked. She wasn't sure how to answer his question. Honestly, she didn't know the answer herself. Remi wanted to believe she'd do the right thing and not just fall into bed with the first willing man she came across, but she couldn't be sure that was true.

"I don't know," she admitted. "I was scared, but that's not an excuse. Besides, we're not exclusive or anything, right?" She knew she was pushing all Tex's buttons. Remi worried that she had pushed him too far.

"We're not exclusive because you won't give us a fucking chance," Texas growled. Remi stared him down as he towered over her. Most people would have been intimidated by the two big alphas hovering over them, but she also knew that the guys would never hurt her, no matter how angry they seemed.

"He's not wrong, Honey," Jag agreed.

"What do you two want from me? I've given you everything you've asked me for. You demanded that I spend the night between the two of you, to stop you from going off and doing something stupid," she spat. Jag's smile was mean and she took a step back from them.

"You telling us you didn't want that, Honey?" he asked. His voice sounded like a cross between hurt and pissed and Remi instantly regretted her comment. The hurt in Tex's eyes had her gut twisting into knots. She owed them both so much more than the pain she was causing them.

"I did," she whispered. "I wanted you both," she admitted. "I still do."

"Tell me about your daughter," Jag insisted. Remi sank down to the bed and didn't hide the sob that escaped her parted lips. Could she do this? Could she share her biggest regret with Jag? Remi had already shared Aria's story with Texas but he was just as broken as she was. He had as many regrets as she did. Jag wasn't like them. He was right—he was different, better almost, but telling him that might hurt him and she had done enough of that tonight.

"I lost her," she admitted. "I should have seen that drunk driver, but I was too busy saving everyone else around me. If I just paid attention, I could have saved my little girl." Remi wiped at the hot tears that spilled down her cheeks. Texas sat on one side of her and Jag on the other. They were always doing that; surrounding her, making her feel safe and even loved, but that was impossible. The three of them had known each other for just a few short months now, but she felt closer to them than she had anyone in a long time.

"None of that was your fault, Remi," Tex offered.

"You won't change my mind, Texas. I know you are trying to help, but I won't ever be okay with what happened to Aria." Jag took Remi's hand into his own.

"And now, you feel that way about your cousin?" Jag asked.

"What?" Remi questioned. "Why would you think that?"

"Because it's true, isn't it? You missed seeing Aylen's abduction and now I'm betting, you feel like there was more that you could have done." Jag said.

"I should have seen Ay being taken instead, I was busy with —" Remi gasped and covered her mouth as if she didn't want to say the rest of what she was thinking. She seemed to hurt the guys at every turn and now was no exception. "I'm so sorry," she said.

"No, I get it, Honey," Jag said. "You were busy saving my ass and if you would have been paying attention to your visions, this wouldn't have happened. Does that sound about right?" It did and that made her feel like a complete ass. How could she want to trade one life for another? She wouldn't. She loved her cousin —Aylen was her blood, her family. But, if Remi was being completely honest, she would tell Jag that she was falling for him and that's why she felt so guilty. She was falling for them both and that wasn't a good idea. She was better alone. Life was easier when she was alone. Remi had less to lose that way and she didn't care if that made her a coward.

"That's not exactly right," Remi whispered. "I'd do that all again," she admitted.

"Come again," Texas said.

"I'd spend the night with the two of you again, even if that meant that Aylen would be taken. For so long I've been scared to chase down what I've wanted. The first night I met the both of you, I knew that I was supposed to end up between you. I saw it—you know, I had a vision, but I was a chicken and pushed you away. I let myself believe that I was better off without you both because if I let you into my world, I could lose you and that would kill me."

"You don't let anyone in, do you Baby?" Texas asked.

"No," Remi admitted.

"That must get pretty fucking lonely," Jag growled. He was right, it did. Remi nodded and Jag pulled her against his body.

"What's changed?" Jag asked. "Why are you giving us a chance now?"

"Because you're not letting me run and hide. You both followed me half-way across the country and now, you're here, asking me to give you a chance." She looked between the two of them and smiled.

"We want you to give us a chance, Honey," Texas said. "I think the three of us can work if we try. Do you really want to try, Remi?" he asked.

She knew the answer to his question before the word even left her lips. "Yes," she murmured.

"Thank fuck, Baby," Jag said. "I've been waiting for you to admit that."

"You're not just saying yes to being with us," Texas warned. "You are saying yes to it all—our dominance and your submission. We want that, Remi. Hell, I need that more than I need air. Can you give that to us?" Remi wanted to tell them yes but giving up her control meant that she'd have to fight her own personal demons daily. How could she do that and come out on the other side, unscathed?

"I'm afraid," she admitted. "If I give you my control, what happens to me then? I can't do this alone. I can't face my past and walk through to the other side."

"You won't be alone," Jag promised. "You have both of us, Remi. Whether you know it or not, you've had us both for a while now. Let us in," he begged. "Let us love you." That was a tall order for her. She had never been in love before, not even with Aria's father. Could she love them both? Remi looked into Jag's blue eyes and smiled. She reached back and took Tex's hand into her own and nodded.

"Alright," she promised. "I want to do this. I want all of it—both of you, the whole nine yards." Jag's smile nearly lit up the room and the heat she felt coming from Tex's body, as he pressed up against her back, felt like it could set her on fire.

"Strip," he whispered into her ear.

"Slowly," Jag added. She stood from the bed and faced both of them. They were watching her and that alone made her feel powerful. She liked the way their eyes followed her every movement. It was hot the way they looked at her like she was their next meal. How had she missed seeing their pent up desires every time they looked at her before? Was it always there?

Jag hissed out his breath when she slowly slid her shirt up over her body, just like he asked. He was enjoying the show and judging from the way his erection was pressing against his jeans, Texas was too.

"Like this?" she teased. She knew exactly what she was doing and the effect she was having on them. They liked to think they held all the power but she could see from the way they looked at her that wasn't true. Remi was the one with the power and she wouldn't trade it for anything. It was a heady rush knowing she could do just about anything she wanted right about now.

"Yes," Texas agreed. He reached for her and she took a step back, teasing him. His frustrated groan filled the small hotel room and she giggled.

"Tease," Jag said, without any real heat. "Now the jeans," Jag ordered. Remi smiled up at him and shimmied out of her skin-tight jeans. She stood in front of them in just her panties and lacy bra, not quite sure if she should try to hide or let them take in every inch of her body. Both guys looked her up and down, hunger in their eyes that told her that she was what they wanted. Remi had her doubts but seeing the effect she had on both Texas and Jag made her hot and ready for whatever they wanted to do with her.

"Um," she stuttered. "What next?" Jag pulled her against his body, Texas framing her other side.

"Are you going to trust us and let one of us be in charge, Honey?" Texas asked. That was a good question. How much of her control would she be able to give over to them? She trusted them both and that counted for so much. Her life was unpredictable and she was damaged. Letting them take care of her just felt right.

"Yes," she confidently agreed. "But, can you both be in charge?"

Jag smiled over at Texas and shrugged. "Probably not," he admitted. "If you haven't been able to tell by now, Tex and I seem to have a power struggle going on when it comes to you, Baby," Jag said.

Remi giggled, "Gee, I haven't been able to tell," she teased. She noticed a fit of new jealousy that hummed through the air whenever she was with both guys at once. Tonight, she hadn't felt that and she worried that asking them both to be in charge of her might tip the scales and send one of them over the edge. The last thing she wanted was to send one or both of them leaving the room, pissed again.

"I don't want that to happen tonight," she admitted.

"We can try," Texas offered. "Right, man?" He looked at Jag and smirked.

"We usually pick an alpha so that there is no confusion or hurt feelings," Jag said. "But, I'm willing to give it a shot, if you are, man."

"So, you'll both tell me what to do?" Remi asked.

"If you'd like that, Baby," Texas offered. Remi slowly nodded and that seemed to be all the consent either one of them needed. Jag practically pulled her up against his body, to kiss his way into her mouth and Remi wrapped her arms around his neck. The three of them were a tangled mess of arms and legs, reminding Remi that she was practically naked between the two of them.

Texas pulled her panties down her legs, leaving her bare to whatever evil plans he had for her. She had to admit, she'd be on board with every one of them. Tex ran his big thumb over the seam of her ass and gently nudged it into her. Remi gasped and pushed back against him, needing more than just his thumb. She loved anal and the thought of having two men sharing her body, at the same time, completely turned her on.

"Fuck," Texas growled. "When you do shit like that, it makes me crazy, Baby."

"I need more, please," she begged.

"Have you ever tried anal?" Texas whispered into her ear.

"Yes," she hissed.

Tex chuckled against her skin and thrust his thumb in deeper. Remi cried out his name. "You want one of us to take your ass and the other to take your sweet pussy?" Texas asked. Remi could barely speak past her consuming need for them to take her in every way that they wanted.

"Yes," she whispered.

"Shit," Jag said. "Baby be sure. Once we do this, you won't walk away from us again. This is your last call, Honey. You in or out."

"In," she agreed. "All in." Remi pushed back against Texas' big hand and liked the way he hissed out his breath, reminding her that she still had some power in all this. Texas swatted her fleshy cheek with his free hand, causing her to yelp.

"Stop trying to take control," Tex warned. He pulled his thumb free and Remi whimpered, causing him to laugh. "Yeah, now you're getting it, Honey," he said. Texas grabbed his overnight bag and headed into the bathroom, appearing seconds later with a tube of lube. "Let's get that hot ass of yours lubed and ready while Jag takes your pussy." Jag smiled at her and she knew that he was more than ready to follow Texas' lead. He unhooked her bra and shucked out of his clothes, sinking down onto the bed.

"Straddle me, Honey. You're going to ride my cock and give Tex access to that glorious ass of yours," Jag demanded. She didn't hesitate, doing exactly as he asked, sinking down onto his erection, inch by delicious inch. He felt so good, she had to still once fully seated on his cock to get back some of her tightly held control. With these two, Remi felt anything but controlled and that scared and thrilled her all at the same time.

"You feel so fucking good, Baby," Jag groaned. He pulled her down and kissed her mouth like he wanted to devour her. Jag didn't let her up for air when Texas started to work his lubed up fingers in and out of her ass, getting her ready. Jag nipped and licked her lips as her breathy little sighs and moans escaped from the pleasure they were both giving her. It was almost too much and at the same time, not enough. Remi needed more.

"Please, Tex," she moaned as he worked a second finger into her ass. "I can handle you, please," she assured. Remi knew that Tex was a big guy, but this wasn't her first time experiencing anal. She knew how the searing heat led to the most extreme pleasure she had ever had and that's exactly what she needed right now. Texas pulled his fingers free and ran his shaft down the seam of her ass. Remi couldn't' help herself, pushing back against him, as if in invitation.

"This is going to be hard and fast, Honey," Texas growled. He nudged the head of his cock into her ass and she ground against Jag, opening herself to both of them. Texas slid the rest of the way into her ass and stilled.

"Fuck," Jag swore. "She feels so full with you inside her ass. The sound of their breathing filled the room and when both guys started to move, she couldn't help the moan that ripped from her chest. Remi let them take over, consuming her and giving her what she needed. It felt like she was floating and she never wanted to come back down. Texas and Jag pumped in and out of her body, finding a rhythm that had her coming, shouting out both of their names. Remi wasn't sure where they ended and she began and she didn't give a fuck anymore. They were one and she was theirs, whether they wanted her or not. It wasn't something she could control anymore—it just happened. She was ready to let her guard down and ready to share her life with someone else. Well, in this case, two someones. God help her, she was falling for them both and the crazy thing was, she wasn't scared anymore. Remi knew that both guys would be there to catch her and that thought alone sent her heart soaring.

Texas and Jag found their releases and the three of them fell onto the bed together. Remi was surrounded by sweaty, hot men and that was just fine with her. They wrapped their arms and legs protectively around her body and she snuggled into them both, knowing that she had finally found where she was supposed to be.

"One thing, Baby," Jag said around his yawn.

"Anything," Remi breathed. She meant it too. She'd do just about anything for the two men who were laying on either side of her.

"No other men," Texas said. She was always in awe of the fact that Tex and Jag seemed to be more connected than her and her twin sister.

"Yep," Jag agreed. "You are ours now. You belong to me and Texas. No more men—no one else touches what's ours. Say you'll be ours, Remi," Jag ordered. She smiled up at him cupping his face to gently kiss his lips and then repeated the same with Texas.

"Deal," she agreed. "I'm yours, Jag. Both of yours."

## TEXAS

Tex woke to the banging on their hotel room door and he nearly jumped out of his own damn skin. "Open this fucking door," a man's voice shouted, pounding on it again for good measure. "I know you're in there, Nena."

"Nena?" Remi questioned, sitting up and wiping the sleep from her hazel eyes. "Who's looking for Nena?"

"No clue, Honey," Jag whispered, pulling on his pants. He shot Texas a concerned look and he had to admit he felt the same way. Why would someone be pounding on their hotel room door, looking for Remi's twin sister?

Texas tossed his t-shirt to her. "Put this on, Baby. We'll find out what's going on," he ordered. Remi tugged his shirt over her messy hair and nodded. Jag pulled his gun from his overnight bag and nodded at Tex, seeming to ignore Remi's gasp.

"What the hell?" she questioned.

Jag shrugged and smiled, "I like to be prepared," he admitted. Texas didn't have a permit to carry, since he had served time, but knew how to handle himself. He pulled the knife that he carried from his own bag and flanked Jag's side.

"Shit," Remi breathed. "You two brought a fucking weapons arsenal," she accused. Jag chuckled and pulled the door open, leaving the safety lock in place. Texas liked that they seemed to be on the same page when it came to Remi's safety.

"Can we help you, man?" Texas asked. The big guy on the other side looked about ready to murder someone and Tex sighed. The guy looked through the small opening at them as if trying to size them up.

"Two of you?" he questioned.

"Yeah," Jag said. "So, how about we handle this like civilized guys and you just leave us the fuck alone."

The guy growled and Texas knew that this little confrontation wasn't going to be as easy as they were hoping for. "Nothing about me is feeling very civilized right about now, Chief. How about you tell Nena that I'd like to talk to her."

"Nena isn't here, Hawk," Remi said. She was standing behind them and Texas made a mental note to talk to their woman about sneaking around like a damn ninja and letting the two of them handle shit like this. He tried to tuck her behind his body, but she wouldn't allow it.

"I'm good," she whispered to Tex. Remi unlatched the door and pulled it completely open. "Come on it," she offered, making a grand sweeping gesture with her arms.

"What the fuck, Baby?" Jag asked. "I thought we explained how things were going to work, here," he growled.

Remi smiled at him, going up on her tiptoes to gently kiss his mouth. "You can put your weapons away, guys. This is Hawk. Nena and I have known him our whole lives and he wouldn't do anything to hurt me. I'm assuming that extends to my two friends, here?"

Texas turned around to stare her down, "Friends?" he barked. "We aren't your fucking friends." The thought of Remi already diminishing what they had promised to each other, pissed him off. He wasn't her fucking friend. Hell, he wanted her to be his wife, but that was something the three of them needed to work out. He and Jag had friends that did the whole sharing gig and they were in happily committed relationships with their Old Ladies.

"You're our ol'lady, Babe. Whether you like it or not, that's how it is now," Jag said.

Remi smiled, "You mean like Lyra is Tank's ol'lady? I thought you had to be married or something."

"We'll get to that," Tex grumbled. "But no, we don't have to be married for the club to accept you as our ol'lady. We'll make it official as soon as we get back to Reckoning." They would too. He and Jag knew that letting Remi into the club, without being tied to them both, would be a huge mistake. The guys would have no problem trying to poach her from them and Tex didn't want to have to beat the shit out of any of his brothers. Especially since he thought of each of the guys as his brothers.

"While this is all real touching; I need to talk to Nena," the guy still standing in the doorway interrupted. "I think she's in danger."

Remi gasped and Texas wrapped a protective arm around her. "Why would you think she's in trouble, Hawk?" she asked.

"I heard you two were in town, asking about Ay and I think that the people who took her aren't happy that you are both sniffing around. Folks in town know what you guys can do and I think it got back to the wrong people that you were looking for your cousin."

Remi's laugh sounded mean. "Well, those assholes took the wrong woman. You know why we're targeted, right?" she asked.

"Targets for what?" Jag asked.

"For human trafficking," Remi said. "Native American's are targeted by traffickers for many reasons," she began. "They like the way we look, our skin tone, they even go as far as to call us exotic."

"Mother fuckers," Texas swore. He had known a few traffickers while he was locked up in the state penitentiary, but he never thought much about the victims.

"Exactly," she said, seeming to agree with his vulgar assessment. "That's exactly what they are, but there's not much we can do to stop them. You see, the other reason we are targeted is that we are almost invisible to the higher powers who can stop this from happening. We are targets because so many of us live at or below the poverty level. People in my tribe are afraid to speak up, believing they will be next if they do. We are expendable and traffickers use that to their advantage and take innocent young girls and women who no one will miss."

Jag wrapped his arms around Remi's other side and she shrugged them both off, taking a step towards the guy she called Hawk. "Well, you know what? I'm not going to stay quiet. I won't let them take my little cousin. She is missed and Nena and I will find her." Tex loved their woman. She was fierce and God help the person who underestimated her strength and visibility.

Hawk had the good sense to take a few steps back and hold up his hands, as if in surrender. "I get that, Remi. I'm on your side. You know how I feel about Nena," Hawk said.

"How you felt about my sister. As I recall, you were the one who walked out on her, Hawk." Remi stared him down as if daring him to disagree with her and damn, Tex felt bad for the guy.

"I still feel the same about her, Remi. That hasn't changed," Hawk said, dropping his hands back down to his side. "Please," he whispered. "Just tell me where I can find her. I need to see that she's alright, with my own two eyes."

Remi sighed, "As far as I know, she's back at Anali's house. She left the bar the same time as I did, last night. I'll try her cell."

"Might as well come in," Jag offered, Shoving his gun into the waist of his jeans. Hawk eyed the two of them, stepping into the small room, shutting the door behind him. Remi found her cell phone and tried to call Nena.

"No answer," she almost whispered. She dialed another number and dramatically exhaled when someone answered. "Anali?" She put the call on speaker and the older woman's voice filled the room.

"Who were you expecting to answer, Remi?" her grandmother asked.

"Did Nena make it home last night?" Remi asked.

"Yes," Anali answered. "Which makes one of you. What were you thinking, staying out all night?" Remi slumped to the bed and shook her head. The last thing Texas or Jag wanted was for her to feel bad about spending the night between them.

"That was our fault," Jag said. "We weren't thinking, sorry." Tex sat down next to Remi and she snuggled against his side.

He loved the way she had taken to using them both for comfort. It was so nice to know that she wasn't going to take off on them again. She even seemed to lean on them and that was exactly what they both wanted from Remi—her trust.

"Well, I remember how it was to be young and in love," her grandmother said. "I guess I can let this one slide—for now. As long as you three promise to come for breakfast this morning and bring Hawk with you," she said.

Remi giggled. "Wait, how did she know he's here?" Jag asked.

Hawk smiled. "Anali knows everything," he said. "You guys are going to need to get used to that if you want to be a part of Remi's life." Texas wanted to tell the guy that they were already a part of her damn life, but now wasn't the time or place to get into all of that.

"We'll be there, Anali," Remi promised. "Just keep Nena at the house until we do," she said.

"Alright," her grandmother agreed. "See you soon." Remi ended the call and Hawk turned to leave their room.

"I'll let you three get dressed and meet you down in the lobby. If you don't mind me tagging along, it would make me feel better to see that Nena's alright, for myself," he said.

Remi nodded, "Thanks, Hawk. Just go easy on my sister. She's been through a lot."

Hawk turned and smiled back at her, "We all have, Remi," he said. Texas watched as the big guy left, pulling the door shut behind him.

"I can't wait to hear this story," Jag said.

"Later," Remi promised. "First, I need a shower. Then, we need to figure out just who wants to hurt my family and why they took my cousin. I'm done hiding like a coward. You two in or out?" she asked. Yeah, Tex would be the first to agree that Remi in charge was a scary woman—and he was completely turned on by her.

"In," he and Jag almost said in unison.

# JAG

They didn't waste time getting showered and dressed, to head back to Remi's grandmother's house. It had been a damn long time since he felt so satisfied and hell, maybe he'd even call it complete. Yeah, that made him sound like a fucking romantic pussy, but he didn't give a shit. Remi agreeing to finally belong to him and Tex felt like it set his whole damn world right.

Remi's Anali was standing on the front porch, just where they left her the day before and the sight of her had to make him smile. She was as fierce as her granddaughter and that said a lot since Remi was the most badass woman he ever laid eyes on.

Nena joined her grandmother on the small porch and Hawk cursed from the back seat of the rental. "You alright back there, Hawk?" Remi questioned. She had ridden shotgun with Texas and Jag and Hawk rode in the back.

"Yeah," Hawk grumbled. He sounded anything but fine but that was none of Jag's business. He knew it was best to keep his nose out of Nena's affairs, or lack thereof. From the way Nena was staring Hawk down, the poor bastard wasn't going to know what the hell hit him, by the time she got done with him.

"Does she look pissed, or is it just me?" Tex asked. Jag knew that Texas was giving Hawk shit, but their new friend didn't seem to have a clue.

"Yeah," Remi agreed. "My sister is pissed. She has good reason to be though, doesn't she, Hawk?" Remi looked back over her shoulder and stared Hawk down as if daring him to contradict her.

"Not now, Remi," he spat. "I can only handle one angry Nez woman at a time." Remi's giggle filled the car and Texas shook his head at her.

"Is there anyone you don't give shit to, Honey?" Tex asked.

"Nope," Remi confirmed. "Let's have breakfast. I'm betting there will be quite a show with our meal," she taunted. Hawk groaned and opened his door to slip from the back seat. Jag watched as he approached the house and Nena as if he was afraid a bomb would go off with every step.

"Anali," Hawk said. He nodded at Nena and slipped his hands into his jacket pockets. Nena didn't return any courtesy of greeting the poor guy and Jag almost felt bad for him.

Texas whistled low behind Jag. "Man, he must have really fucked up," he murmured. Remi shushed him and took Jag's hand, standing between the two of them.

"How about we concentrate on how pissed off Anali looks to see me with both of you. You both have more to worry about than my sister mean-mugging her ex. Jag looked the older woman over and realized that Remi was right—she looked pretty angry at the three of them. Her grandmother couldn't seem to take her eyes off the way their hands were joined and Jag suddenly regretted agreeing to join everyone for breakfast.

"Good morning, Ma'am," Texas said. "Nena," he added.

"I'm not a Ma'am," Remi's grandmother insisted. "Please call me Anali."

"Anali," Jag nodded. "Thank you for having us to breakfast."

"I figured it was the only way to see my granddaughter and we have a good deal to discuss. Nena had a vision last night and we think we know where Aylen is," she said, getting right to the point.

"You do?" Remi let go of both of their hands and ran up onto the porch. "That's great."

"No," Nena disagreed. "It's not great. They are going to move Ay if we can't get to her first."

"Who's they?" Remi asked.

"I have no idea," Nena admitted. "Let's just call them the bad guys. I'm guessing they're human traffickers and they are planning on moving Aylen tonight." Nena didn't hide her sob and poor Hawk looked just about beside himself, trying to figure out what to do next. Jag could tell the guy wanted to go to Nena and soothe her but he also looked smart enough to know that was a shitty idea.

"Then we find her before they move her," Anali said as if it was going to be that easy. "Let's eat breakfast and come up with our plan. We have to change the outcome of Nena's vision and if anyone can do it, it's my girls."

"Where did you see her, Oryana?" Remi asked.

Nena shrugged, "You aren't going to believe this but they're moving her to New Orleans. I saw her last night and she showed me they were on the move. I saw road signs and if I'm not mistaken, it's the same route we traveled here. Whoever has her is taking Aylen to NOLA. She told me to hurry, that they said something about getting back to town by tomorrow afternoon."

"That doesn't give us much time," Remi said. "Do you know where they are taking her, once they get to New Orleans?"

"I think so," Nena said. "But it's going to sound crazy."

"Try us," Jag asked. Since meeting Remi and her sister, crazy seemed to be their new normal.

"I think they are taking her to a bar called Tito's," Nena said.

"Tito's?" Texas asked. "Why the hell would they take her there?" Jag knew that place and the MC that met there. They were bad news and the guys at Reckoning usually steered clear of them.

"I'm not sure, but I think whoever is buying her set the meeting location. I saw that bar and it reminded me of the one where your club meets." Nena said.

"Fuck," Jag swore. "Buy?" He knew that they had suspected Aylen had been taken by traffickers, but hearing that theory confirmed sucked.

"Yes," Nena said. "Ay said that they have a buyer for her and that she's supposed to be delivered to the parking lot of some bar in New Orleans."

"I'll call Tank to let him know," Tex offered. "I can't believe that any of our guys would buy a woman, but that doesn't mean it isn't possible. I'm hoping that whatever's going down doesn't involve Reckoning. Hell, we still have a mole in the club, but things have been so quiet lately, I thought maybe that was over."

"A mole?" Hawk asked.

"Yeah," Texas confirmed. "Someone ratted out our Prez's woman and her sister for being seers and put everyone in danger."

"Were you in danger, Nena?" Hawk growled. Tex shot Nena an apologetic look.

Nena turned on Hawk, pressing her finger into the poor guy's chest. Jag could almost feel the sexual tension between the two. "That isn't any of your business anymore, Hawk," Nena spat.

"Come on Oryana," Hawk groaned. "You can't keep shutting me out like this. I made a fucking mistake and I've owned it. Are you ever going to fucking forgive me?"

"No," Nena breathed. Hawk backed down and Jag honestly felt bad for the guy. "I won't forgive you—I can't."

"Why not," Hawk asked. "Give me one reason why you can't just give me another chance, Nena."

"Because I won't let you hurt me again," Nena whispered. Hawk growled and ran his hands through his hair.

"Maybe we concentrate on finding your cousin and then you two can have a private conversation," Jag offered, clapping Hawk on the shoulder. "Emphasis on the whole private thing."

"Fine," Hawk barked. "I'd like to help find Ay if that's okay with you," he asked Nena. She nodded and turned back to Remi.

"What are we going to do?" Nena whispered. Remi looked to Jag as if she was looking for some help and he smiled, pulling her into his arms. Jag knew firsthand, how hard it was for Remi to ask for help or give up her control. The fact that she was turning to him for help felt damn good.

"How about we get Tank and the guys involved, like Texas said, and you let us fly you back to NOLA. I'm betting we can beat Aylen back home and use the element of surprise in our favor."

"I think that sounds like a good plan," Remi's grandmother agreed. "As long as you two promise to keep my granddaughter's safe."

"Three," Hawk corrected. "If that's alright with everyone." Texas and Jag looked at Remi and then Nena. They both nodded their agreement.

"Fine," Jag said. "We leave in an hour. Eat up and we'll head for the airport as soon as you'll are finished."

"Thank you," Remi said. "I really appreciate you flying us all home." Jag pulled her back against his body and Tex crowded into her side.

"We'd do anything for you, Honey," Jag whispered into her ear. "Anything." Remi giggled as he kissed his way down her neck. Texas swatted her ass and gave her a quick kiss.

"He's not wrong, Baby," Texas said.

****

They got back to New Orleans by the mid-afternoon and headed straight to the bar. Tank had called in all the guys to help Remi and Nena. Lyra and Beth were both waiting for them and when Tank called everyone to church, the women agreed to head over to Tank's place. He loved the way Remi seemed to fit right into their club. Hawk offered to go with the women, to keep them safe and Jag had to admit—he liked the guy. What he really enjoyed was watching the way Hawk's presence seemed to make cool, calm Nena squirm. It was going to be a good time, watching the two of them circle each other, but Jag was sure Hawk would find a way to handle Nena—one way or the other.

"So," Tank said, trapping Jag and Texas into the corner where they were both drinking beer and playing darts. "You two making it official with Remi?" he asked. Jag looked at Texas, wanting to follow his lead with the three of them coming out. It wasn't really that big of a deal that he and Texas shared women. They had done it for so long, it was just accepted in their little club. When they first started doing it, rumors flew around that they were together too. Jag usually didn't give a fuck about shit like that but Texas set the record straight, letting everyone know that the only thing he and Jag shared was the woman between them. The guys seemed to drop it after that and when he and Texas took a woman up to their room, no one even looked twice anymore.

Texas shrugged, "Yeah," he said, his goofy, lopsided grin in place. Jag couldn't help but laugh. Texas' good mood was infectious.

"She seems to make the two of you happy," Tank said.

"She does," Jag admitted.

"Great, so how about you two announce Remi as your woman tonight? The last thing I need around Reckoning is you both having to bust some heads because another biker is making moves on your woman," Tank grumbled. He wasn't wrong. If anyone even thought about laying a hand on Remi, he and Texas would rip the guys hand off—brother or no brother.

"Judging from that mean look on your face man, I think Tank might be onto something," Texas said. "How about we make it official tonight after church?"

"Done," Jag agreed.

"Great," Tank said. "I'll text Lyra and tell her to get her ass back over here later. First, we handle business and then I plan on giving my wife her MC name."

"Wow," Texas said, "That's great. What prompted this?" Usually, when a club member introduced his ol'lady to the rest of the guys, he'd give her a name. Beth became "Seer". Reaper gave her that name when he made her his.

"I know she's been wanting a name," Tank said. "I see it every time we call her sister, "Seer," I just hope she likes what I came up with."

"I'm sure she will, man," Texas said.

"You guys come up with one for Remi?" Tank asked. Jag and Texas both looked at each other and smiled.

"Raven," they said in unison.

"We haven't really discussed it with her though," Texas admitted.

"It suits her," Tank said. "Let's get this meeting over and then we can call the women back over," he said. "Everyone listen up," he shouted over the hum of guys drinking and playing pool. It wasn't quite a full house tonight but there were still enough guys there to hold a meeting and if necessary, take a vote.

"We've got trouble again and this time, Remi needs our help. Her cousin has been taken and we have intel that whoever has her is bringing her back to New Orleans." Tank paused and looked around the room and Jag found himself doing the same. As VP, he was supposed to have his Prez's six and right now, that included looking out for the traitor who seemed to stay one step ahead of them. They had a plan in place and if it worked, they'd finally know who their mole was. Jag, Tex, and Tank met after they landed, out at the airport. Tank agreed to pick them up and that way, their little meeting could remain a secret. It was the only way they could be sure that no one had ears or eyes on them. It sucked that they couldn't trust their own guys, but taking chances with their women again, wasn't an option any of them wanted to entertain. Tank had almost lost Lyra and he knew the score. If they didn't find a way to bring down their mole, they'd never find a moment's peace. It was time to end this crazy cycle and shut down whoever wanted to hurt them.

"We believe that Remi and Nena's cousin is going to be delivered to Tito's bar tomorrow night," Texas said. The three of them had decided to feed the club just enough information and hopefully, they'd be able to weed out the traitor. Tito's housed another area club—the Perdition MC.

They had a small handful of guys that Jag knew they could trust with not only their lives but Remi's too. We're working with the local authorities to bring down this new ring of traffickers that has popped up. Seems like Reap's old boss wasn't the only game in town." Jag watched the room as the muffled curses rang through the crowd. He felt the same way about having to deal with scum bag traffickers and potential club traitors. He was ready for a little bit of normalcy after everything the club had been through—first with Beth, then Lyra and now, Remi and Nena.

"We need a few volunteers to go with Texas, Jag and me, over to Tito's to talk to their Prez. I don't want any trouble between our two clubs but if they're a part of this trafficking ring, that's exactly what we'll give them. We can't stand by and allow scum like that in our town; especially now that it's touching our women," Tank said. He was right. If the traffickers were after Native American women, Remi and Nena might never be safe and that wasn't something he could stand by and let happen. He'd do just about anything to keep Remi safe and Jag knew that Texas felt the same way.

A few of the guys raised their hands, volunteering to help out and by the time the meeting was over, they had a plan in place that would keep Remi safe and find her cousin. He also hoped that the club's mole would take the bait and run to snitch. That was where Reaper would come in. Tank had convinced everyone that Reap was out of town and wouldn't be back for a few days. Reaper was hiding out, waiting for whomever their rat was to show his true colors and try to sneak over to Tito's. Once they figured out who their snitch was, they would be able to hopefully find Aylen. Jag knew that they were playing a dangerous game but what choice did they have? He knew his woman well enough to know that she wouldn't rest until they found Aylen. Jag just hoped like hell that they weren't too late.

## REMI

Remi sipped the wine that Beth handed her. She wanted to be out looking for Aylen, not having girl time with her closest friends. The only silver lining in all of this was having front row seats to watch how uncomfortable Hawk could still make her sister. Nena had been through so much with him and Remi knew that her sister wasn't quick to forgive. She'd especially have trouble forgiving the man who was the cause of her trust issues. Nena spent most of her adult life chasing the relationship she had found with Hawk, only to turn down every man who offered her more. Remi wasn't sure if her twin sister was truly disinterested in every man she crossed paths with or a masochist—waiting for Hawk to beg her for another chance. Either way, he was here now and if Remi was reading the signs right; he wasn't planning on going anywhere any time soon. And, even though Nena had thrown up her walls and looked like a complete sour puss about it, Remi could swear that her sister was happy to have Hawk tagging along.

Nena sighed and took a sip from her own wine glass. "Please stop looking at me like that Remi," she begged. Nena turned to look out the front window to where Hawk stood like a sentry, guarding the four of them.

"How am I looking at you, Oryana?" Remi taunted.

"Like you are enjoying all of this way too much," Nena spat.

"Well, since we're talking about the hot guy you guys brought back with you," Lyra started.

"We aren't talking about him," Nena hissed.

"Oh, but I think we are," Beth agreed with her sister. "Listen, this is my first time out of the house in weeks. I need the details," she begged. "My entire life has become deciding which breast pump I need to buy; which stroller is the easiest to open and which car seat is the safest. I'm up to my eyeballs in baby stuff and I need a break. I literally have about two more minutes until I'm going to have to pee again and I demand to know more about the handsome guard dog out there. Have pity on this new mama-to-be and spill it." Lyra giggled, palming her own enormous belly and Remi knew that Nena was doomed. There was no way her sister was going to win this argument.

"I can't wait to meet him," Remi said, patting Beth's belly, hoping to change the subject for Nena's sake.

"No," Beth said. "No belly rubbing for you. Not until I find out who the hottie is and why Nena keeps giving him the stink eye."

Nena groaned and dramatically rolled her eyes, causing them all to laugh.

"Being pregnant has made you mean, Beth," Lyra chided. "But, I'm with my sister on this—spill the details, Nena."

"Fine," Nena said. "I dated Hawk in high school and it didn't work out. End of story." Remi barked out her laugh and Beth and Lyra looked at her like she lost her mind.

"That is not the end of the story," Remi chided. "He put you through hell and you let him."

"Please, Remi," Nena begged. "I don't want to rehash this now."

"Fine, but you need to decide what you want, Nena. He's not the same man he used to be. Hawk has changed and maybe you should give him a chance. You deserve to be happy." Hawk walked into the kitchen from the porch and stopped when he realized all eyes were on him.

"Everything alright in here, ladies?" he asked.

"Yep," Remi said. "We were just talking about girl stuff," she added.

Hawk winced and shuttered, "Well, Jag just called my cell and he'd love for you all to join them, back at Reckoning. Apparently, the meeting is over."

"Church," Beth corrected. She stood from her chair and grabbed her purse. "And, if you fucking hurt our girl Nena again, you'll have to deal with me." Beth pointed her bony little finger into Hawk's chest as if driving her point home.

Lyra giggled and shook her head, "Yeah—you're definitely meaner since getting pregnant." Remi laughed and tagged along with Beth, wanting to check in on Lyra's daughter, Delilah, before they headed back to Reckoning.

"We'll check in on Lil and tell the babysitter we're leaving," Beth called back to her sister.

"Thanks," Lyra said.

\*\*\*\*

Hawk drove them back to the bar and Lyra filled them in on her news—she and Tank were going to announce that they were having a boy tonight. Remi felt a bittersweet joy for her friend and her happy news.

"Reaper and I are going to name our little one Chris," Beth announced, rubbing her belly.

Lyra giggled, "Tank and I aren't half as prepared as you and Reap," she said. "I'm not sure if this kid will have a name by his first birthday, at this rate. It took forever for Tank to agree to know the baby's sex. I explained to him that as a seer, I already knew. When he realized that it's nearly impossible for me to keep a secret, he reluctantly agreed to let me tell him. Now, the big oaf is over the moon at the idea of having a son. He said that I've already given him a daughter, so a son feels right."

Hearing Beth and Lyra talk about what they were going to name their sons made Remi's heart flip flop. They went on about newborn babies—their little wiggles, smells, and squeaks. Remi realized that she had forgotten what it felt like to hold a newborn baby and she wondered if she would ever hold one of her own again. Being with Texas and Jag made her want things again that she hadn't for so long. The thought of having another baby both terrified her and felt right, all at the same time. Remi wondered if the guys had ever given a family much thought. The three of them were all so brand new to each other, bringing up the topic of relationships and babies, might be too much.

By the time they got back to Reckoning, she was feeling all the self-doubts creep back in and Remi knew that her next step would be to put her walls back up. As soon as she walked into the bar, both her guys were by her side.

"Hi," she squeaked.

"Hey," Texas drawled. He kissed her like it had been days since they saw each other and not just hours. Jag did the same thing as soon as Tex finished with her and when he lowered her back down his body, she could feel every delicious inch of his erection.

Jag framed her face with his big hands and the way he looked at her; Remi knew he could tell exactly what she was thinking. "Don't," he growled.

"Don't what?" Remi questioned, although she knew exactly what he was warning her against.

"Don't put your fucking walls back up, Baby." Jag ran his thumb over her bottom lip and she could feel it tremble.

"I—I can't," Remi stuttered and ran from the bar. She noticed the stares of disapproval and pity as she walked past the other bikers. That was the last thing she wanted—letting them see her cry, but she couldn't seem to control her fucking emotions.

"Shit," she heard Texas curse over the hum of guys drinking and having a good time. Remi wasn't stupid, she knew she wouldn't be able to run far and that sooner or later, Texas and Jag would catch up to her and demand answers. But, she needed these few seconds as her reprieve to get her emotions under control.

Remi found a quiet spot in the corner of the dark parking lot and wiped at the hot tears that spilled down her face. "Fuck," she shouted into the air.

"My thoughts exactly," Jag barked, rounding the corner from the front of the bar. Remi looked around, trying to find some retreat, but there was none. She was going to have to face her guys, like it or not.

"Want to tell us what that was all about?" Texas questioned. Remi stared the pair of them down and shook her head.

"Come on, Remi," Jag taunted. "You changed your mind? I thought we went through all of this, already." The last think Remi wanted was for either of them to believe she had changed her mind. That just wasn't possible now. She wanted them both too much and maybe that's what this was all about—her fear. She was afraid of letting them in and afraid of losing them, all at the same time.

"I'm scared," she whispered. There, she could give them some pieces of the truth and hope that would be enough for now.

"Of us?" Texas asked.

"No, of course not," she said. "You would never hurt me—physically."

"You're worried we will hurt you, though. Aren't you, Remi?" Jag asked.

"Yes," she admitted. She wiped at her wet cheeks again, hating that they were seeing her this way. She never let anyone see her vulnerability. It was her rule and one she hated breaking.

"I'm afraid of giving you both that power over me, but I think it's too late," she said. "I've already let you have my power and my heart."

"And, you're worried that we'll break it?" Jag asked.

"Yes," she said. Admitting that was the hardest part.

"Would it help if I admitted that I've fallen in love with you, Remi?" Jag asked. "And that I'm just as scared as you are?" Jag pulled her against his body and she hesitantly let him.

"How about if I admit that I've done the same, Baby?" Texas asked. He framed the other side of her body, wrapping his arms around her waist. "Because I have. I love you, Remi. I think I have since the night you walked into Reckoning to warn Lyra."

"Really?" she whispered. Sobs racked her body and she wished she could get the crying under control. Remi sniffled and let out the breath she didn't know she had been holding.

"Yep," Texas agreed.

"How about you start trusting us a little, Honey? I promise your heart is safe with both of us," Jag said. Remi smiled through her tears and nodded.

"I think I want more kids," she blurted out. Yeah, that wasn't really the way she planned on springing that on them, but there it was, out in the open. She would forever miss her little girl, but she wanted to find a way to free herself from the burden of guilt she was carrying around with her. She'd never be able to find a way forward with Tex and Jag if she held onto her past and let her grief and guilt consume her. They were right, she deserved more. She deserved a chance to be happy with them both. It was time to grab for the brass ring and hold onto it with both hands.

"How many more are we talking?" Jag asked.

Remi shrugged. "I haven't given that much thought. But, just watching how happy Beth and Lyra are, I think I'd like to have another baby." Remi swiped her hands through the air as if trying to erase her words when neither guy made a move to agree to her crazy plan. "Never mind—just pretend I didn't say any of that last part."

Texas turned her to face him and smoothed back her unruly hair with his big hands. "I'd like kids too, Baby," he said.

"You would?" she stuttered.

"Yep," Texas admitted and kissed her.

Jag spun her around to face him and tugged her back up his body, kissing his way into her mouth. "Same, Honey," he said after he broke their kiss. "So, you agreeing to be ours, officially then?" he asked.

Remi didn't hesitate, nodding her consent. "Yes," she said. "I'm yours Jag. And, yours, Tex."

"Great," Tex said. "Let's get this part over with so we can find your cousin and start making babies." Texas hoisted Remi over his shoulder, placing his big hand on her ass when she protested and tried to get him to put her down.

"I'd hold still, Honey," Jag ordered. "Tex is on a mission and you never stop a man with a plan." She looked up to find Jag following behind Texas, grinning like a damn lunatic. Texas carried her into the bar and stood her between him and Jag. All eyes were on them, from Tex's whole caveman routine, and Remi felt like she wanted to run and hide again. This time, Jag kept a hold of her, as if he could read her mind.

"Hey guys," Jag yelled over the crowd and everyone grew silent. "Remi is with us, now." There was a cheer that rang through the bar and Remi bit back her giggle.

"Jag and I are sharing her and she's agreed to marry us—both of us," Texas said, smiling down at her.

"I did not," she loudly whispered int his ear.

Jag swatted her ass, causing her to yelp. "Sure you did, Baby. Just now, in the parking lot. You told us you were ours and that means, you agree to marry us."

"Jag," she said. "I can't marry both of you."

Jag shrugged, "Maybe not legally, but we can work all that out later. You're ours now, Remi." He pulled her in for a quick kiss and the cheers grew louder. When Tex did the same thing, the guys held up their beers to toast the three of them. "We've also decided on her name," Jag yelled over the crowd.

"What is it?" One guy called from the bar.

"I already have a name," she insisted.

"It's customary for us to give you your MC name," Texas offered. Remi crossed her arms over her chest and Texas laughed. "Yeah, this whole giving up control thing is hard on you, isn't' it, Baby," he teased.

"Raven," Jag breathed, kissing her forehead.

"You like it?" Texas asked.

"I do," she admitted. Her grandmother used to call her that. It felt right that her guys gifted her that nickname too. "I love it."

"Good," Texas drawled. "This is Raven," he said. The club members cheered again. Tank and Lyra stood beside them and Tank hugged Remi.

"Raven's one of us now," Tank said. "Welcome to Reckoning, Raven." She nodded and hugged Lyra, feeling her friend's sadness. It was something that they could do with each other. Whenever she touched Beth or Lyra, she could tell exactly how they were feeling and right now, her friend was feeling rage and so much sadness, it almost made Remi's heart hurt.

"Lyra?" she whispered into her ear.

"Not now," Lyra pleaded. She gave Remi a smile but she could tell that Lyra wanted to do anything but smile. "I'm fine," Lyra lied.

Tank pulled her back against his body and wrapped his hands around her belly. "While we have everyone's attention," Tank shouted over the unruly club members. "Lyra and I also have an announcement to make." Lyra smiled up at her husband and nodded. "We're having a boy." Tank kissed her cheek and the whole bar erupted into one big celebration that seemed to go on forever. After a few minutes, Tank held up his big hand, to hush the crowd again. "I've also decided on Lyra's MC name."

Lyra looked up at him and burst into tears. "Tank," she sobbed.

"I'm sorry it took me so long, Honey," he said. Remi couldn't help the fresh wave of tears that now coated her cheeks, watching the two of them together. "I just didn't want to fuck it up —you know?" Tank asked.

"You won't," Lyra choked. "I know you won't fuck it up, Tank."

"Mystic," Tank whispered into Lyra's ear. He was just loud enough for Remi to hear her friend's new name. She had to admit, it fit Lyra.

She nodded and Tank smiled down at her. They were truly beautiful to watch together, seeing all the love they had for one another.

"Mystic," Tank called out to the bar. Another round of cheers and toasts sounded through Reckoning and Remi wondered if she'd ever get used to the MC life. She had a feeling that would be her learning curve, but one she'd willingly figure out. Belonging to Texas and Jag left her little choice and she was fine with that.

# TEXAS

Texas and Jag spent the night with Remi between them, up in their room above Reckoning. It was decided that they'd stay in town for a bit until things could be settled with Aylen. Tonight, they'd either find Remi's cousin or discover just who their mole was. Either way worked for him—Tex was spoiling for a fight. It was just his nature to want an eye for an eye and he definitely wanted to fuck up whoever took Remi's little cousin.

Just before Remi and Jag were awake, he heard a soft tapping at their door. He and Jag had a strict "do not disturb" policy in place. If someone was knocking at their door, it better be damn important.

He pulled on his jeans and opened the door to find Reaper and Tank on the other side. "Fuck," he whispered. "It's important, isn't' it?" Tex grumbled.

"Yeah, sorry man. I think this is something Jag's gonna want to hear too," Tank said.

"I'm up," Jag grouched.

"Me too," Remi sat up and yawned, forgetting that she wasn't wearing any clothes.

"Shit, Raven," Tank yelled. "My wife will have my balls if she knows I just saw that." Remi giggled and covered herself with the sheet.

"Sorry guys," she said. Texas made a mental note for him and Jag to have a talk with their girl about boundaries while they were at Reckoning. "How about I get dressed and meet you downstairs?" Jag stood and pulled on his jeans, leaning over the bed to kiss Remi.

"Don't be long, Honey," he said.

"Promise," Remi agreed. "I'll be right behind you."

They sat at the table closest to the bar and he and Jag helped themselves to some much-needed coffee. Jag sat down across the table from Tex and they both looked expectantly at Tank. "Let's just have it," Jag growled.

"Well, I was going to at least let the two of you drink your fucking coffee," Tank grumbled. "Sorry to wake you so early but we have some intel you need to hear."

"Let's hear it then," Remi said, bouncing down the stairs to join them. She stood over the table and put her hands on her hips, trying to look badass but to Tex, she passed for sexy as fuck. Jag pulled her down onto his lap and laughed when Remi protested, squirming around on his lap, slapping at him. Texas could tell the whole scene was turning Jag on too.

"You keep wiggling that sexy little ass of yours on my lap and this meeting will be over. I'll haul you over my shoulder and carry you up to our room again," Jag promised.

"Fine," Remi spat and stilled. "Let's hear this news."

"I think I know who our mole is," Reaper said. "He's not one of our guys but he's connected to Reckoning."

Texas didn't like the way this was going. They had always just assumed that the traitor was inside the club. "Who?" Texas asked.

"It's a guy named Ringer. He's my ex-business partner's son," Reaper said.

"The one who took Chloe and then ended up being on our side?" Tex asked. He and Brick had gone to Texas, to help Ringer keep an eye on Sophie when things went down with Reap's boss, Anthony Sr. Tex thought for sure Ringer was on the up and up. From the way he took care of Sophie, he'd even bet the guy was in love with her. Sophie gave him shit at every turn and Ringer didn't seem to care—if that wasn't love, Tex wasn't sure what was.

"I didn't have him pegged as a traitor," Texas said. Reaper looked about ready to tear him or anyone else apart for getting in his way.

"Well, I found that asshole hanging around Tito's in Perdition MC leathers. It can't just be a coincidence that he shows up now, out of the blue, after staying away from NOLA for so long. He's been gone for months and he's what—just back? It's too much of a coincidence," Reaper said.

"Okay," Jag broke in. "Let's say this guy is our mole. How do you explain that he wasn't even in town during the whole ordeal with Lyra and Tank? I just don't think it adds up. Texas said he seemed like a good guy," Jag added.

"Thanks for throwing me under the fucking bus, man," Texas grumbled.

"No problem," Jag shot back.

"Enough," Remi demanded. "You two can bicker like old women later. Right now, I'd like to hear what Reaper has to say. My cousin's life depends on it."

"I think we need to head over to Tito's," Reaper said. "I've had intel that your cousin will get there in about an hour. We can find Ringer and question him. I'm done trying to figure his ass out. Just when I think I can trust him; the shit always seems to hit the fan."

"Sounds good," Remi said, standing. Texas pulled her back down to his lap. There was zero percent chance that either of them was going to let her just tag along on this little mission.

"No," Jag barked. "No fucking way are you going with us." Remi tried to stand and Tex banded his arms tighter around her waist.

"You can't stop me from going to save my cousin, Tex. In case you have forgotten, this was my rescue mission and I'm allowing you both to tag along," Remi yelled. She squirmed to get free form his lap and Tex let her up. She wanted to have this argument here and now, and there would be no stopping her. Remi was a force when she wanted to be.

"It's going to be dangerous," Jag said. Texas and I can't just let you walk into something like that."

Remi barked out her laugh, "I think you're forgetting who I am and what I do, Jag. I've been in worse jams."

Yeah, I remember finding you tied up in that paper factory," Texas said. "If I remember correctly, Jag and I saved your sassy little ass."

Remi shrugged, "Okay, that was one time. You can't both hold that against me for the rest of my life."

"No," Texas agreed. "But you'll have a nice long life, with us, if you fucking obey us and stop giving us so much shit for wanting to keep you safe."

"I'm sure we can all come to some kind of compromise," Tank offered. "How about we let Remi tag along and you two keep an eye on her. It would be good to have her there in case her cousin needs her—you know, a familiar face." Texas hated the idea of dragging Remi back into danger but what choice did they have. From the stubborn look on her face, Texas could tell that he and Jag were fighting an uphill battle.

"Fine," Jag agreed. Tex shot him a look like he had lost his mind and he had the nerve to smile. "She's not going to back down and we're running out of time."

"Come on, Tex," Remi begged. "Just give me a chance to prove that I can handle myself." Jag was right—they had no other choice.

"Fine," he spat. Tex pointed at her and she smiled. "You stay with either me or Jag the whole fucking time," he ordered.

"Of course," she quickly agreed.

"Let's head out," Tank said. He and Reaper stood. Remi took Tex and Jag's hands. It's going to be fine," she promised. Texas worried that there would be no way for her to keep that promise.

****

It was just past ten in the morning when they got over to Tito's. Traffic was crazy and the Perdition's bar was clear across town. Remi seemed to become more distracted with every passing moment and Texas worried that she was going to drive herself half-crazy with worry.

"It's going to be alright, Baby," Jag promised.

"Don't make me a promise you can't keep," Remi said. "Aylen might not be alright and I'm going to have to face that fact."

"How about you just try having a little faith," Texas said. "Is that the van you saw in your vision?" he asked, pointing to the white van that sat in the back of the bar's parking lot.

"Yes," she said. Remi pulled free from her seatbelt and tried to crawl over Tex's lap, to get out of Tank's truck.

"Where the fuck you think you're going?" Tex asked.

"To get Aylen out of that van," Remi said.

"No," Reaper said. "No one leaves the truck until we figure out what the fuck Ringer is doing and who he's talking to." He pointed to the back door of the bar, where a guy with dark hair and tattoos that covered both of his bare arms was talking to a woman who looked a hell of a lot like Remi. Tex knew the guy was Ringer and if he had to guess, the woman was Remi's cousin.

"Aylen," she whispered. "She's alive."

"If your cousin is being held against her will, why isn't she bound? Look—" Texas pointed to the pair, who looked to be having a deep conversation about something. "She's not being held against her will at all. No ropes or duct tape, like you saw in your vision."

"You're right," Remi said. "Why isn't Aylen trying to run or fight? She's free."

"Let's let it play out and see where this goes," Tank ordered. Remi sat back in between him and Jag and watched Aylen out the front window of the pick-up. He was right, Aylen and Ringer looked to be having a deep discussion about something or other and Tex wondered how her cousin even knew the guy. Remi said that Aylen had never been out of New Mexico. How would she know some guy from NOLA? Remi looked like she was about to demand they let her out of the truck when a tall man walked out of the bar and pulled Aylen against his body. Her cousin willingly let him wrap his arms around her waist. Aylen was letting the man touch her and from the way she looked up at him, she wanted it.

"What the fuck?" Remi swore. "What the hell is going on here?"

"That's a damn good question," Reaper agreed. "Let's find out." They all got out of the pick-up and crossed the parking lot. As soon as Aylen saw Remi, she ran to meet her cousin.

"Remi," Aylen said. "Please don't be mad."

"Mad?" Remi asked. "Why would I be mad? I'm so happy to see you. Are you alright? Did they hurt you?"

"I'm fine and they didn't hurt me," Aylen promised. "I wasn't sure what was happening but now I understand. I'm so sorry that I put you and Nena through all this. But, I'm fine. I'm going to be fine." Remi looked past Aylen to where Reaper was pinning Ringer up against the back wall of the bar.

"How are you connected to this?" Reaper shouted. "What the fuck does this have to do with you?"

"I'm prospecting with Perdition," Ringer said as if that would explain what he was doing back in town. "I'm just trying to help out my Prez, Rios here. Ringer looked over to Perdition's president and Texas worried that there was going to be trouble between the two.

"I know who Santiago Rios is," Reaper said. "How do you know Aylen?"

"I think the question here is how do you know my Aylen?" Rios asked.

"Your Aylen?" Remi questioned. She turned to Aylen and held up her hands. "What the hell does he mean, calling you his Aylen?"

Remi's cousin shrugged, "I guess exactly what it means. I'm his," Aylen said.

"Because he bought you?" Remi asked.

Aylen barked out her laugh and Texas worried that they were going to leave Tito's without Remi's younger cousin. It didn't seem that the woman wanted to be saved by Remi or anyone else. She wanted to be just where she was and that might break Remi's heart.

"You don't understand, Remi," Aylen said. "You never will, and that's alright. I think it's time for you to leave, cousin." Aylen turned and Remi grabbed her arm. "Let go, Remi," Aylen growled.

"Or what?" Remi asked. "This isn't you, Ay. You're the sweetest, kindest person I know. Don't turn your back on me, Aylen." Texas hated hearing the pain in her voice. All he wanted to do was protect her but he had a feeling he wouldn't be able to save Remi from the heartbreak of losing her cousin.

"Aylen," Remi sobbed. "Think about Anali and your mom. Think about our family," she begged.

"I am—you are all I'm thinking about, Remi," Aylen promised. "Please, I know what I'm doing."

Texas wrapped his arm around Remi's shoulders and she turned to sob into his chest.

"Baby," he crooned. Jag pressed up against her back and wrapped his arms around her and the three of them stood like that, her cocooned between them for what felt like forever.

Tank cleared his throat, "Um, I hate to break this up guys but we should be going. Nena has tried to call my cell a half dozen times and she'll want to know what's going on here."

"What the hell do I tell her?" Remi asked. "I have no idea what's happening. This is crazy." Ringer came back out of the bar through the back door. "I know you don't trust me, Reap," he started.

"No, I don't," Reaper agreed.

Ringer laughed and nodded, "Right. Well, I just want you to know that Aylen isn't in any danger. She's Rios' ol'lady—nothing and no one will touch her."

"Is that a threat?" Reaper asked. He stood nose to nose with Ringer and Tex put Remi behind him and Jag. If there were going to be punches thrown, he didn't want her anywhere near the guys.

Ringer held up his hands, as if in defense. "Nope," he said. "I'm just letting you know that she's safe, is all."

"Like my sister was safe with you?" Reaper spat.

"Whoa now—Sophie was always safe with me, Reap. I—I'm in," Ringer stuttered and for a minute, Texas wondered if the guy was going to admit that he was in love with Reaper's little sister. For all their sakes, he was hoping the guy was smarter than that. "How is Soph?" Ringer whispered.

"Sophie is none of your fucking business," Reaper said. "Stay the hell away from her and we won't have any problems." Reaper turned to walk back to Tank's truck. "Oh and Ringer, that was a threat," Reaper said, over his shoulder. Ringer shook his head and walked back into Tito's.

"Let's go, Honey," Jag ordered.

"I can't," Remi insisted. "I can't just leave Aylen here."

"You heard Ringer," Baby," Tex soothed. "She wants to be here and she's safe. There isn't anything we can do to stop this from happening. We need to go fill Nena in and figure things out from there. It'll all work out," Texas promised.

"No, it won't but I appreciate you trying to make me feel better. You're right, I can't force my cousin to listen to reason but this isn't over," Remi shouted as if she was hoping Aylen could hear her. Texas wondered what they were missing. Something wasn't quite right but he couldn't put his finger on it. One thing was true, this was far from over. For now, he just wanted to find some sort of normal that the three of them could settle down into. The rest would work itself out.

## REMI

Remi waited for the guys to get home from church. She had spent the whole day at work, reorganizing the children's section at the library and the last thing she wanted to do was go back into town with the guys. Remi insisted that they go to Reckoning and have a good time but knowing her guys the way she did, Remi knew that they would be back to their little cabin just as soon as the meeting was over. That gave her just enough time for a bubble bath and a glass of wine.

It had been just over a month since she found Aylen. Remi had seen her cousin around town and every time she ran into her, Ay pretended not to notice her. It was getting old and Remi wasn't sure if she had much more fight left in her. After their meeting, she found Nena and told her about the strange encounter with their cousin. Nena said that she had a vision, the night before, and she believed Aylen was telling them the truth. For now, Nena convinced her to drop the whole thing but running into her cousin around every corner only had her anger amping up to new levels.

The guys had convinced her to move in with them. Jag and Texas had a great cabin, just outside of town, not too far from

Tank and Lyra. Remi decided to move in there and make it their home. They even remodeled the master bedroom and adjoining bath, to make sure they had enough room, for the three of them. Remi loved them for trying to make her feel as if life was moving forward, as normally as possible. That included making her keep her promise to marry them both.

Their commitment ceremony was beautiful. Tank performed the ceremony and even though it wasn't legally binding, it was absolutely perfect. They pledged to love her and keep her safe for the rest of their lives and she knew that Texas and Jag meant every promise. They were her warriors, her knights— although she'd never admit that to either of them. And now, she was hoping that they would agree to be the fathers to her babies. It was their next step and one Remi hoped they would both be ready for.

She had hoped to get home earlier in the day, to prepare a nice dinner. Jag called her and told her they were bringing home pizza and that was fine with her. She heard them come home just as she was slipping from the bath. She threw on her robe and went to find her guys.

"I'm telling you that you're wrong, man," Jag said. "Angelo's makes the best pizza."

"You guys having a tiff?" Remi teased.

"We do not have tiffs, Honey," Texas growled. "We're having an argument over who makes the best pizza in town."

"Oh well, that's easy," Remi said. "It's Ma's. They make the best pizza in NOLA. I see we're having Angelo's?" She eyed the pizza as if it had done her wrong and Jag laughed, pulling her in for a kiss.

"How about you tell us how your day was and I'll order Ma's for you?" Jag asked. Texas grumbled something about Dino's Pizzeria being the best in town and Remi rolled her eyes and giggled.

"I got the children's section all worked out today," she said. "I can't wait for the kids to see it." Just a few months ago, she avoided that section like it had the plague. Every time the kids would come in for story time, she'd cringe. She had even gone as far as to hire a part-time high school kid to come in and read to the little ones.

Now that she had Jag and Texas in her life, that all seemed to change. She realized she was looking forward to seeing the toddlers and their parents come into her library every week. Now, she felt hope instead of such crippling despair.

"That's great, Honey," Texas said. Jag ended his call with Ma's Pizzeria and tossed his cell on the kitchen counter.

"We should celebrate. How would you like to do that, Honey?" he asked, pulling her against his body.

"Um," Remi squeaked. "By making a baby?" she asked. The cabin fell quiet and Remi thought she could hear her own heart beating.

"A baby?" Jag asked.

Remi suddenly felt uncertain. Maybe it was too soon, but that was the way this thing between them seemed to work—at warp speed with no breaks or airbags. "Are you sure you're ready for that, Baby?" Texas asked.

Remi shyly nodded her head, letting her long, dark wet hair fall into her face. Jag gently stroked it back from her eyes, framing her face with his hands. She held onto him like he was her lifeline. They both were.

"Tex and I have already talked about this, Honey. We're ready whenever you are. We were just waiting for you to give us the green light, Remi. If you want this, then let's make a baby."

"Really?" she asked. She could feel the hot tears fill her eyes before she felt them falling down her cheeks.

"Yes," Texas said. "We want it all with you, Raven." She liked the way Texas had taken to using her MC name. It felt so personal every time they called her that. It was the name they had given to her and every time they called her their Raven, she felt loved—even cherished.

"All?" she questioned.

"Yep, a family," Jag said. "A house full of kids."

Remi giggled. "How about we start with one and work our way up from there?" she asked.

"Deal," Jag agreed.

"So, Raven," Texas drawled. "What are you seeing for our future?" he asked.

"Everything," Remi said. "I see everything with you and Jag, Texas. I love you both so much."

"We love you too, Baby," Jag said. "Now, how about we start working on those babies?" Remi giggled and eagerly ran for their bedroom, her guys hot on her heels. She really didn't predict the future but Remi was beginning to see that her assessment was promising. Her guys were her world, her life—her everything. And, that was a future she was looking forward to.

## ORYANA

Oryana Nez ran into the dark alley, knowing full well that outrunning whomever or whatever was after her was probably not an option. She was tired, hurt and if she wasn't mistaken, losing enough blood that she'd be dead within the next thirty minutes. She had tried to call for her sister, but it was nearly impossible to clear her mind enough to focus. Their minds couldn't communicate if she let all the worry and confusion cloud her thoughts. Nena was out of luck and just about out of time but running was all she had left.

She ducked into an open doorway and whispered a little prayer of thanks that she found a door that was unlocked. It looked like an old warehouse and with any luck, would have plenty of hiding places. She found a room that was in the darkest corner of the building and slid under a rusty old desk, pulling the squeaky chair in to meet her body, effectively trapping herself. Nena hoped that whoever was after her had given up the hunt but from the months he spent tracking her, that was just wishful thinking.

Nena focused on her breathing and calming her loud, shallow breaths. If someone tracked her into that room, her breathing would give away her location. She closed her eyes and opened her mind, calling for her twin sister, Remi. They were both seers and shared a special connection. Her grandma used to call it their twin telepathy, making them both giggle; but she was spot on. Her grandmother knew of their abilities, being a seer herself. They came from a long line of women with the gift and Nena was well trained in how to use her abilities.

"Remi," she silently called to her, using her mind. "I need your help."

Nena heard someone rummaging around in the outer rooms of the warehouse and she knew it was only a question of when they'd find her. Her only hope was her sister finding her and time was running out. She cupped her bloody side and hissed out her breath at the throbbing, painful wound. Nena hurt all over and she wondered just how much longer she'd be able to hold on. Judging by the amount of sticky moisture that coated her hands, she didn't have long.

"I'm not sure she's in here, man," she heard a male voice say. "Where else could she have gone?" another man asked. Nena didn't recognize either of their voices. She strained her ears to listen to their conversation, trying to access how close they were. If she wasn't mistaken, they were just outside of the room where she was hiding and she was doing everything in her power not to make a single sound.

"Maybe she doubled back and took off. We need to get back before we're missed," the other guy said. "We've wasted enough time looking for someone who doesn't want to be found." Nena wondered just what he meant by that. Why would she want them to find her? Nena strained her ears to listen for any signs of the two men entering the room she was hiding in.

"Let's go." Nena heard the command and she felt like she was holding her breath waiting to see if they were actually going to leave and give up their search. When she heard them walking away from her, down the long corridor that led back to the alley, she let herself finally breathe. Nena pulled out her cell phone, praying that she'd have some service, but she didn't.

"Shit," she whispered, slipping the phone back into her pocket. "Remi, I need your help," she sobbed. She knew that help wasn't coming for her—not this time. Her twin sister was always the stronger of the two of them. Remi was the one who took charge in situations that called for them to be brave. She was the one who had Nena's back and that was how she liked things.

Nena didn't dare move from her hiding spot, afraid that the two men looking for her weren't really giving up. It was quiet, dark and cold. The old warehouse smelled like urine and mildew, telling her that it must have been abandoned for some time. If that was the case, no one would find her. She would need to find her own way out, sooner or later but fear paralyzed her and the thought of climbing out from under the desk made her sick. Nena closed her eyes and let the darkness consume her, focusing on her breathing. She needed to get herself under control and not let her anxiety take over. Nena just needed a few minutes to get herself together and then she'd find her way out of the cold, dark warehouse. Where she'd go next was the issue, but she'd find somewhere to lay low until she could figure out who was after her and why. The last thing she wanted was to involve her sister and new friends at Reckoning in any of her mess, but she had no choice. Nena knew what she had to do but showing up, unannounced at Hawk's place meant that she was going to have to eat shit and apologize for being such a bitch to him. Sure, she could do that if it meant not involving her sister, but she was certain he wasn't going to make her apology easy for her to choke out.

# HAWK

Hawk Acosta had never been a man to do things on the fly but relocating his entire life from New Mexico to New Orleans felt like a pretty big fucking deal. He did it to follow a woman and that made him sound like a complete pussy, so he kept that little bit of information to himself. When people asked why he was picking up and leaving the only home he'd ever known, he just told them he had a job opportunity he couldn't pass up. It was partially true but what most people didn't understand was that he could live just about anywhere since he worked from his home. He was a business consultant to some of the biggest corporations in the U.S. He was the one they'd call in to fix problems that most deemed unfixable. He loved what he did because it usually involved kicking some ass until everyone was whipped back into shape. The Dom in him really liked that part and the rebellious biker side of him got a kick out of people in power having to take orders from a kid who was born on the wrong side of the tracks.

Yeah, he'd done well for himself, but this latest chapter in his life had him feeling like he was going out of his fucking mind. Following the woman of his dreams half-way across the country probably qualified him as a fucking lunatic, but he really didn't care anymore. He wanted her and not taking what he needed felt wrong. He'd waited a damn long time for her to give him a fucking chance and he was done sitting around, hoping for that to happen.

After a shit day of dealing with everyone wanting something from him, all Hawk wanted to do was fall into bed and dream about the sexy seer who filled his nightly dreams. Oryana Nez was his walking wet dream, although he'd never tell her that. They were high school sweethearts. Hell, she was his first everything, but that was a damn long time ago. He fucked up and cheated on her, during their senior year and she never forgave him. He'd asked her out a half dozen times, only to be turned down each and every time. She'd give him one hell of a hard time if she knew that he had fantasized about having her naked, willing body on top of his, panting out his name, every night since the last time she turned him down.

Hawk told her that he'd leave her alone until she came crawling back, begging him to take her out on a date and she let him know, in no uncertain terms, that would happen when pigs fly. He hadn't seen any flying pigs lately but coming home to find the sexy brunette on his front porch was certainly a surprise. She was huddled up in the corner by the front door and when she spied him getting off his bike, the fear he saw in her beautiful brown eyes nearly did him in. Something or someone had hurt Nena and his inner caveman came roaring to life. He wanted to tear whoever or whatever it was that made her so afraid, completely apart.

He hurried to his front porch and looked her up and down. Nena made no move to get up from her spot in the corner and he towered over her. "What happened?" he demanded. Nena wiped at the tears that spilled down her cheeks and he cursed himself for being such an asshole. She didn't need his demanding ass questioning her. She needed to be comforted and held, but Hawk knew from his past experiences with her that she was a bit prickly when it came to stuff like feelings.

"Fuck," he whispered, noting the blood that covered the left side of her shirt. Nena was hurt and had lost a good deal of blood. "Don't get pissy, Nena, but I'm going to touch you." Her eyes widened and for just a minute, he thought she was going to protest. Instead, when he knelt to assess her wound, she let him. He ran his big hand gently down her side and she hissed out her breath

"Please, Honey," he begged. "Tell me what happened so I can help you," he whispered. "Who did this to you?"

"Someone is after me," she sobbed. "I've been followed and I don't know who it is or what they want. When I was trying to get away, I tripped and fell onto a metal rod. I didn't know it was this bad but when I pulled free from it, there was so much blood."

"Are you sure someone is after you, Nena?" he asked. Hawk knew that Nena and her twin sister, Remi were seers, but beyond that, he didn't really understand much about their abilities.

"You calling me a liar, Hawk?" she questioned. She tried to pull free from his hold, but she was too weak. "I knew it was a mistake to come to you," she said. Her words felt like a physical slap.

"Now you're just trying to piss me off, Nena," he accused. "How about you start from the beginning and tell me what happened. Then you can treat me like shit and accuse me of being an asshole."

"I didn't do either of those things," She defended. "I simply said that I shouldn't have come to you with my problems. If you let me go, I'll just find someone else to help me."

"No," he growled. Nena gasped and stilled.

"What do you mean, 'no'?" she asked.

"I mean, I will help you. You don't need to go to anyone else." Hawk could feel the tension rolling off her slim body. "First, I'm going to call my friend, Doc and he's going to come to take a look at you. I won't chance taking you to the hospital, not if someone is truly after you. While he's patching you up, I'll call Tex and Jag to let them know what happened.

"No," she practically shouted. "I can't involve Remi. She just found out she's pregnant and I won't put her or her new little family in danger. If someone wants to hurt me, they'll use my family to get to me. I need to know who's doing this before we call in everyone else for help."

He knew that she was right—someone was trying to hurt her and all he wanted to do was help her. Nena had taken the first step and met him at his house. It was his turn to give her a little in return. Maybe then she'd stop fighting him at every turn and even let him in a little. That was all he really wanted—just a chance with Oryana and then he could take what he wanted from her—everything.

The End

**Hawk (Reckoning MC Seer Book 4) coming soon!**

**Bonus sneak peek of BE Kelly's next new series -**

# Ringer (Perdition MC Shifters Book 1)!

## **RINGER**

Ringer rode his bike into the corner of the lot, not wanting to attract too much-unwanted attention. He was laying low and showing up at Reckoning wasn't his smartest idea. But, if he wanted to talk to Reaper, he knew where to find him. The little dive bar was Reap's hang out and home to his club. Ringer always used to feel a pang of jealousy when he thought of Reaper being a part of something that he'd give his left nut to join.

He had been a lone wolf until he found the Perdition MC. Finding any group to belong to seemed like a pretty far-fetched idea to him. Ringer never seemed to fit in, but that wasn't his fault. He had to keep a part of himself separate from everyone he ever knew or trusted because once the truth came out, they would never look at him the same way again. That's why he had to end things with sexy little Sophie Payton, Reaper's younger sister.

About six months ago, she agreed to Ringer's crazy plan, to let him take her out of NOLA and stow her away someplace safe. He told her it was the only way he could keep her safe from his scum bag father but that was a total lie. Ringer was really hoping to get her out of town, away from her older, very over-protective big brother, to get his chance with her. Reaper didn't like or trust him and he couldn't really blame the guy. If he had a kid sister that fell in love with an asshole like him, he'd be pissed off too.

Sophie made it very clear that she wasn't interested in him—in that way, but the mixed-signals she sent him left Ringer in a perpetual state of confused and hard. Just before the local authorities in NOLA caught his father and charged him with human trafficking, he thought he had finally broken through her defenses. Sophie had agreed to one night with him and he was sure his dreams of owning the sexy little vixen was finally going to happen, but he was dead wrong.

They spent the night tangled up in his bed sheets and when the first light of morning broke through the curtains at the cheap Texas motel they were hauled up in, he found the bed empty. Sophie had ditched him, without a word and he couldn't decide if he was more pissed or hurt by that. Ringer got dressed and rode his bike around that small, broken-downtown, looking for his woman but there was no sign of her. She was gone and he was left in the middle of nowhere, wondering what the hell he did to cause her to just take off.

After two days of searching, he finally gave up looking for her and headed back to his little motel room to figure out his next move. He went back and forth between telling Reaper he lost his sister, to just disappearing from the face of the earth to avoid the beating Ringer was sure to get from Reap. He wasn't a coward and he wouldn't take the easy way out of this or any situation, for that matter. When Ringer finally got up the nerve to dial Reaper's cell number, he was surprised to learn that Sophie had shown up back in NOLA the day after they hooked up. And, maybe that was all he was to her—just a hookup. He wanted to be more for her, but Ringer wasn't about to crawl back into town and beg her for another chance when he didn't do anything wrong in the first place.

Ringer decided to stay in Texas for a bit. He had nothing waiting for him back home—is old man was in prison for trafficking and the woman he wanted didn't want him. His father's business interests were left to him and he and Reaper were now co-owners of the textile company their fathers had started together. He told Reaper he wanted nothing to do with the company, signing his half of the business over to Reap and wishing him all the best. Ringer needed a fresh start, but that wasn't exactly what he found. So, he headed back to New Orleans to confront Sophie, but he was a giant fucking chicken.

He had been back in town for a little over a month now and still couldn't find the courage to face the woman that he had fallen in love with. He had a run-in with Reaper after he got back to town. Hell, if that's what you could call it. Really, it was more like Reap still trying to blame him for everything—his father, the business, and even Sophie. How could he explain to Reaper or Sophie that he was back in town because he didn't know how to stay away from her anymore? How did he tell Sophie that he felt like he was being drawn to her the way a wolf is drawn to his mate? She couldn't be that to him because if he let her into his life, it would be the end of hers. He couldn't be with Sophie and the sooner he realized that, the better.

Once he got back to NOLA, he became a regular at a little dive bar in town called Tito's and was prospecting to join the club that met at the bar—Perdition MC. Ringer even found a house to rent that wasn't like the shit-hole motel he was in with Sophie. Staying in a motel only reminded him of the hot night they spent together and the fact that she so easily tossed him aside and went back to her life in New Orleans. It hurt and he wasn't sure he'd ever get past her walking out on him, even with the countless women he fucked to occupy his nights. They were nameless, faceless bodies to lose himself in but he was never sated. Ringer was beginning to realize the only way to feel that again would be to find Sophie and demand to be a part of her life again and knowing Sophie, that wouldn't work well in his favor. She was tough as nails and determined to shut him out of her life. There would be no getting through to her, even if he was up for trying.

He couldn't give her what he wanted either. That would mean letting her into his life and his secret. He wasn't sure how she'd get past him being who he was and that realization was his biggest factor for keeping his distance. How could he explain that he was a shifter and with every full moon, he had to lock himself up in a storage container to keep from hurting anyone? He was a wolf—a lone wolf, destined to be by himself for the rest of his life, like it or not.

## SOPHIE

Sophie Payton pulled into Reckoning's parking lot, not sure how she was going to explain her bulging belly or the fact that she could no longer fit into any of her jeans, to her older brother, Reaper. Her OBGYN told her she was lucky that she hadn't started showing months earlier. She was almost five months pregnant and one hundred percent positive that the baby was Ringer's. When she agreed to one night with him, she never imagined it would lead to a lifetime commitment to a kid, yet here she was—pregnant and alone. She didn't tell anyone about the baby; none of her friends and especially not her big brother. Reaper would want to find Ringer and tear him apart, but what good would that do? He'd feel better but she'd still be alone and facing the realization she was going to have to not only bring the kid into the world but raise him or her alone.

Tonight was the night she faced the music. Tonight, she got dressed in the only thing that fit her—yoga pants, and an oversized t-shirt, and drove her pick-up to Reckoning. It was home to her brother's MC and honestly, her home too. His club had adopted her as their own kid sister. She knew that sooner or later the overly protective bikers would all find out that she had gone and gotten herself knocked up. Telling Reaper was her first step and then she'd face the rest of them. Hiding in plain sight wasn't an option for her any longer. This baby had other plans for her and forcing her hand to make an announcement she wasn't ready to make, was a crap move. She'd blame Ringer for everything but honestly, none of this was his fault. She was the one to run away and that was the problem. Getting close to Ringer wasn't a part of the plan and letting him in, for even a night, felt reckless and daring but she knew how it would end. Men left—all of them and she wasn't about to sit around and wait for Ringer to change his mind about her. Better to get out before losing her heart completely to the guy.

Besides, he didn't come running back to town after her, when she took off. He even sold his half of the company to Reaper and that felt like the final slap in the face to her. If Ringer wanted to send her a message, she got it loud and clear. He didn't want her and he proved that every day that he stayed in Texas.

Sophie checked her reflection in the rearview mirror and sighed. "Whatever," she mumbled and pulled free from her seatbelt. She had her mission—find Reap and break the bad news that she was carrying Ringer's baby and beg her new sister-in-law, Beth to help her pick out some maternity pants that actually fit. Beth was pregnant too, as was her sister, Lyra. Between the two of them, she'd be able to get the scoop on where to pick up maternity clothes cheap. She also needed to start planning on what she was going to do once the baby got there. She worked alongside her brother, at their father's textile company and she loved her job and working with Reaper. She hoped that after he got over the initial shock and anger of her pregnancy, he'd let her keep working there and maybe even bring the baby in with her, to avoid the costs of daycare. But, she was getting ahead of herself. Telling her brother was her first step and she just needed to rip the band-aid off and get this part over with.

Sophie walked into the bar and nervously looked around for her brother, bumping into every big, tattooed biker along the way. She found Reaper sitting with Beth at the bar and she exhaled. She almost wanted to giggle at her own theatrics but finding her sister-in-law there was a good omen. Beth would be able to keep Reaper from flying off the handle and going off to do something stupid—like having a giant tantrum and going off to kill Ringer. If she was lucky, Reaper wouldn't even ask who the father was, but she knew her brother well enough to know he'd ask. He made it his mission to know every bit of her business, claiming that's what big brothers did. She liked to tell him that only nosey, older brothers butted their noses in where they weren't wanted or needed and he'd usually roll his eyes and ignore her.

"Hey guys," she almost whispered. They didn't hear her over the music, so Sophie tapped them both on their shoulders, getting their attention. "Hey." She waved and Reaper stood to hug her. She had taken the last week off, claiming to be sick, but she was just hiding. Once she started showing, she panicked and hid away in her little rental house that belonged to Beth.

"You feeling better, Sis?" Reaper questioned. She was careful not to let her little baby bump touch him when he pulled her against his body.

"Yeah," she lied. "Just a little bug." If only he knew that her little bug was actually a baby, he might not be so welcoming. Beth smiled and grabbed her, pulling her into a bear hug of her own. As soon as her sister-in-law pushed her away, she knew that Beth had guessed her secret. She was a seer and had an uncanny ability to see anything and everything about Reaper and Sophie. It was how Beth and Reaper met—she had dreams about him her whole life and she found him. Hell, Beth saved Reaper and her and they were damn lucky to have her in their lives. Although, Sophie didn't feel so lucky at the moment. Beth's powers only grew stronger and she was starting to be able to get vibes from people just by touching them and Sophie could see it in her sister-in-law's eyes that she knew about the baby.

"Um, I need to talk to you both," Sophie stuttered.

"Shoot," Reaper said. "We're all ears."

"No," Beth said. "I think we should talk about this up in our room." Beth and Reaper kept a room over the bar, for nights that they wanted to stay in town. They also had a perfect little cabin just on the outskirts of town that Sophie considered to be paradise. Sophie wanted to just blurt out her news and get it over with, but Beth was right, some privacy might be the best call for telling Reaper.

"Why do we need to go up to our room to talk?" he asked Beth.

"Because Sophie has something she needs to tell us and it's a private matter," Beth said.

"Hmm," Reaper hummed. Whenever he made that noise in his throat, Sophie knew that he was sorting through things in his mind. It usually ended with a screaming match between both her and her brother and this time might be no different.

"Please, Reap," Sophie begged. He looked her up and down as if sizing her up and when his eyes got to her belly, they stopped. Sophie tried to cover her belly with her hands, turning away from his stare but it was too late—her brother had caught on and there would be no retreat or privacy for the conversation they were about to have.

"You're pregnant?" he growled. Her brother's impeccable timing was spot on. The loud music, that usually filled the bar, had stopped and his shout was heard by just about everyone in the room. The dull hum of conversation ceased around them and Sophie felt all eyes on her.

"Yes," she murmured. "I'm pregnant." Sophie closed her eyes as if she could hide that way but she knew that as soon as she opened them again, she'd find Reaper staring at her with so much disappointment it would physically hurt her to look at him.

"What the fuck?" She popped an eye open, knowing that wasn't Reaper's growly voice asking the question. It was a voice she had only heard in her dreams—Ringer. Sophie turned to find him standing behind her, his dark mohawk pulled back in a braid that ran down the center of his skull. She always liked when he wore his long hair that way; she could see all his neck tattoos. Was he really at Reckoning? It had been five months since she left him sleeping in that crappy motel room after they spent their night together. The only night that she was willing to give him—the only night he asked her for. Ringer was beautiful, angry and very much present and Sophie's world felt like it was about to spin off-kilter. She couldn't seem to find her balance and just before everything went dark around her, she heard Ringer's soft promise.

"I've got you, Honey," he said.

**Ringer (Perdition MC Shifters Book 1) Coming in May 2020!**

## About BE Kelly

### Paranormal MC Romance Writer
### Supernatural, flirty, and a little bit dirty!

BE Kelly is a paranormal romance author who enjoys adding in her alter ego's love of MC! She loves all things witches, shifters and you'll maybe even find some vamps in her future! Check out other works by this author under the pen name K. L. Ramsey, for more MC, ménage, and even some contemporary romance.

## BE Kelly's social media links:

**Instagram ->**

https://www.instagram.com/bekellyparanormalromanceauthor/

**Facebook ->**

https://www.facebook.com/be.kelly.564

**Twitter ->**

https://twitter.com/BEKelly9

**BookBub ->**

https://www.bookbub.com/profile/be-kelly

**Amazon ->**

https://www.amazon.com/BE-Kelly/e/B081LLD38M

**BE Kelly's Reader's group ->**

https://www.facebook.com/groups/530529814459269/

# More works by BE Kelly

## Reckoning MC Seers

Reaper
Tank
Raven

# Coming Soon

Hawk

## Perdition MC Shifters

Ringer
Rios

Made in the USA
Columbia, SC
22 October 2021